silence & song

Praise for Melanie Rae Thon

The Voice of the River

"[Thon's fiction] reads like a prayer and sings like a hymn."

—*Billings Gazette*

Girls in the Grass

"Melanie Rae Thon belts out her stories in a tone and style reminiscent of classic blues singers. [...] The reader is swept along not only by her remarkable characterizations, but also by the taut, magic current of her prose, which carries an exhilarating rhythmic punch."

—*The New York Times Book Review*

In This Light

"What is particularly striking about Thon's work, other than her austere, poetic prose, is her attention to detail and the deep knowledge with which she writes every scene. Thon not only does her research; she inhabits her characters."

—*Seattle Post-Intelligencer*

"[Thon's] prose is always blade-sharp, but with a tender lyricism that will draw you from shock to wonder, to awe at the radiant heat of love that Thon finds inside the sorriest of circumstances."

—*Image Journal*

"[Thon] turns her laser gaze toward those among us who walk with the most invisibility, who suffer the most quietly; those whose stories don't make the pages of glossy magazines. [...] Readers of literary fiction will appreciate Thon's careful attention to what these characters have to offer: lessons, warnings, and an odd kind of hope."

—*Foreword Reviews*

"[Thon] is a writer worth reading for her soulfulness and her sensual detail."

—*San Francisco Chronicle*

Sweet Hearts

"Thon writes so searingly ... that the reader is compelled not to judge, but to understand the fragmented and sometimes violent lives she depicts. [...] She knows how to break our hearts."

—*Minneapolis Star-Tribune*

First, Body

"The rhythmic beauty of Thon's writing is everywhere extraordinary: Here is a writer who can really sing the blues."

—*Kirkus*

MELANIE RAE THON

FC2

TUSCALOOSA

The University of Alabama Press
Tuscaloosa, Alabama 35487-0380

Manufactured in the United States of America

FC2 is an imprint of The University of Alabama Press

Book Design: Publications Unit, Department of English, Illinois State University; Codirectors: Steve Halle and Jane L. Carman; Assistant Director: Danielle Duvick; Production Assistant: Mike Shier

Cover Design: Lou Robinson

Typefaces: Centaur MT (Titles) and Adobe Jenson Pro (Text)

⊗

The paper on which this book is printed meets the minimum requirements of American National Standard for Information Sciences—Permanence of Paper for Printed Library Materials, ANSI Z39.48–1984

Library of Congress Cataloging-in-Publication Data

Thon, Melanie Rae.

Silence & song / Melanie Rae Thon. -- First edition.

pages ; cm

ISBN 978-1-57366-053-2 (softcover : acid-free paper) -- ISBN 978-1-57366-857-6 (ebook)

I. Title. II. Title: Silence and song.

PS3570.H6474S55 2015

813'.54--dc23

2015014140

for the ones we love

contents

vanishings

There are three ascending levels of how one mourns:
with tears ~ that is the lowest ~
with silence ~ that is higher ~
and with song ~ that is the highest.

—*Hasidic teaching*

I.

My brother kneels in the back of the Chrysler. Leo Derais, eleven years old: he's skipped three grades: this fall he'll start high school.

He's just made the most astonishing discovery, has seen the evidence and understands at last how time moves at different speeds in both directions. (Was that a stone? Is that a rabbit?)

Appears to move.

Quickly now, before the light goes, he wants our father to see what he sees, the earth close to the car ripping backward (skull of a desert fox, bones of a missing child), everything lost, the past shredded and gone (blink of an eye, stuttering heartbeat) while at the same time, in the same world, a ridge of distant mountains unscrolls, quietly revealing itself, advancing slowly forward.

No matter how fast our father drives, the patient line of stone proceeds, always beyond, always ahead of us.

He's trembling now but can't speak. Time does not exist. Time is perception, the endless rearrangement of things in space, the infinite possibilities of their relationships to one another.

A word will shatter thought: skull, stone, star, rabbit: everything here, now, lost and still to come in this moment. There's no reason why he can't remember the future. Even now the light of stars long dead streaks toward him.

Our father, our pilot, delivers us into a night too beautiful to imagine: blue, blue sky, mountains deepening to violet.

Mother unbuttons her blouse to nurse the baby. Joelle, my sister, eleven months old, eight years younger than I am, my father's bewildered surprise, my mother's joyful mystery, Joelle Derais, so radiant strangers stop us on the street and ask to touch or try to talk to her.

If she were alive now, would she be like me, or still be tempting?

I remember her that day at the rest stop: cheeks flushed, lips rosy, the soft swirl of dark curls at the crown of her head (where I kiss, where I smell you), Joelle, my sister, heavy in my arms, heavy in my lungs, the sweet almond scent of you.

I remember the woman who gasped in the bathroom, whose fingers fluttered as she touched Joelle's warm shoulder. *My God is that child real?* She thought my sister was a doll, perfect porcelain, perfectly painted, someone else's real hair, someone else's silky lashes:

My God how porcelain shatters.

Mother wants to stop in Page, just south of the Utah border, high on this plateau of red rock where a pink neon sign blinks *EZ REST* and a green one warns *DESPERADO'S HIDEAWAY.*

Our pilot won't rest; our desperado won't take refuge.

If time does not exist, there must be a place where I can go, where I can find us, where my sister cries and my brother trembles, where bands of rose and gold and turquoise throb at the horizon, where my father turns back, and my mother forgives him. (Somewhere in the night, while I sleep, this happens.)

Forty years. I have these words. I know these numbers. The morning paper my proof: *Oil Spilling, Bees Vanishing. Five Illegal Immigrants Found Dead, Problem Bear Relocated.*

The headline never says: *Invasive Humans Removed from Bear's Natural Habitat.*

EZ REST: I almost remember the sign flashing all night, the room that smelled of smoke and ammonia.

No. We didn't turn. The blue Chrysler sped into the blue night while the light of stars streaked toward us.

Forty years. I remember the taste of blood and bone, tongue cut deep, front teeth jagged, the smell of gasoline and smoke, something burning in the distance. My father tried to stand but couldn't stand, tried again and then a third time. He disappeared as smoke and came back as fire. His face flared in orange light.

How can both legs be broken?

Yes, everything here, now, again, always: the blue Chrysler ablaze, our bodies flung in the desert, the rearrangement of things, the infinite possibilities, the light of stars, yes, I have never seen so many stars anywhere, an ocean of sparkling light, stars alive and dead streaking toward us.

The baby was gone, the baby was missing. I remember Mother crawling in the sand, trying to find her, saying her name, *Joelle,* howling her name into the blue night all around us, leaving *Jo – elle* vibrating through stone and star forever.

My brother rose up white and naked from his twisted body. He was perfect, so thin and pale I could see right through him. He stooped to scratch the sand with a stick. Later I understood the stick was a bone, one he'd pulled from his body.

So fast, my brother! He drew a lovely looping line crossing and recrossing, no beginning or end, some strange magic: flight of the hawk or snake coiling, a wave of sound inside a stone, breath moving between bodies.

I don't remember the days in the hospital, the nights and days I slept, brain swollen. I remember waking in my bed at home, a deer under the mesquite tree by my window, the shadows of leaves fluttering across her body: a deer in disguise: I heard her breath in my breath, felt warm blood surge through me.

Alive, I was. Even now I believe the deer's blood healed me. Mother played "Clair de Lune" on the piano with her left hand, half a song; the deer breathed in fluttery time, and I breathed with her. Doves sang missing notes, but not the right ones, not Debussy's, some startling rearrangement of sound, every song endlessly new, no matter how many times Mother played them.

Blood surges from the heart and soon returns or doesn't. Forty years. At the Mission one day I watched a man restore the wounds of Jesus, scraping away oil and dirt to paint the openings again, red so red it glowed, wounds so deep blood bloomed violet.

Such love! The painter looked thin as Jesus, scarred too, hurt and hungry. Yes, here, God alive, breath inside a starved brown body. He'd repaired broken thorns and broken fingers; now, as he touched the wounds with his brush, tendons beneath flesh flickered. In a looping line of blue vein, I felt the painter's blood in me pulsing.

So easily the body opens.

Good Samaritan Shot Three Times. The news in the paper today. Hand, thigh, right shoulder. Two fingers lost, clavicle shattered. The wound in the thigh will not stop leaking. Nine pints of blood gone. Nine poured back into you. *Is this possible?* Who are you now, filled and saved by the blood of strangers?

The shadows of leaves become the shadows of hands, doctors' hands inside my brother's body, stitching artery and bowel, touching the soft secret skin inside the belly, hoping to stop the blood, to bring him back, to reassemble a puzzle of bone, pelvis and rib from splintered fragments.

Good Samaritan, I would give you all my blood, lie down with you inside, as I was once inside my mother.

Love surged as song in the womb, the universe here, whole and perfect: blood and breath, whoosh and murmur, vibration in soft bone, my body alive with sound, every cell shimmering.

I don't remember walking in my sleep, leaving our little house, the sound of my heart, my parents' breathing. I do remember waking in the cold pink light of morning, wearing a thin yellow nightgown, white cotton underpants. Bare feet wet from the cold wet grass of the golf course. I remember a shiny raven walking across the green green, speaking to me in his language: *All this waste, all this water. Hohokam,* he said. Warning from the past, memory of the future.

I learned I could wake anywhere: under my brother's bed or miles from home, down the arroyo. I don't remember climbing into a neighbor's house, popping the screen with my small fist, slipping inside the open window. I woke in the kitchen, a quart of chocolate milk in my hand, belly too full, carton half empty. A little finch had flown in with me. I left her there, to take the blame, to be a mystery.

I might walk in the desert all night and wake unsafe in my own bed, legs scratched by thorns, feet cut, sheets bloody. I was never afraid. What more could happen? My brother gone, my sister missing. Dreams were not dreams: dreams opened the night so I could enter. I remember a pulse of wind and wing, hundreds of bats flying toward me, parting to let me pass, bodies so close but never touching: the bats made a hole in the night the exact size and shape of my body.

Migrant bats, illegals from Mexico. Saviors, lovers: they look just like us inside, hearts and veins, bowels and kidneys. They cross the border in the dark: unknown, undetected: so small and light you could hide one in each hand, carry twelve in your pockets.

Your cousins!

Days after conception, the embryo of a bat could be the embryo of a human; but now, in the dark, you perceive mysterious differences. Your fingers can hold pen or scalpel, stone or hammer, but theirs have grown long and fine to hold nothing more than skin, a delicate web of wing between them.

Their bodies are perfect. They smell a wild blooming in the night, so tempting it fills their minds, so potent a taste wafting on wind guides them. Long tongues, long noses: they plunge furred faces deep inside the saguaro's white blossoms.

They care nothing for laws or lines, walls or wires. Nectar tastes as sweet on one side as the other. They take all they can. Smugglers, thieves: they rise, faces dusted gold with pollen.

They do not want your blood; they have not come to harm your children.

They want what we want: one sweet life on earth. Who can blame them? Strange angels! They know not what they do flying country to country, flower to flower. By their hunger they offer life, by their theft restore the desert.

Each one, once only! The pollinated blossom of the saguaro closes before noon, will never again open, but in its secret heart, a sweet fruit begins to ripen.

2.

Good Samaritan! Just today, just this morning, I woke before dawn knowing that while we slept something miraculous had happened. Voices too high to hear left my body trembling.

Yes, it's true: I tasted nectar. Down the arroyo, into the canyon, I flew to the place where saguaro had flowered, each blossom wide as my hand; each one so deep those who enter risk drowning.

I have never known such patience. Sixty years to grow one arm, seventy-five to risk blooming. The saguaro might live two hundred years: if lightning does not strike, if fire does not boil and burst it. If humans do not shoot or sever, axe or steal. If tires do not crush. If wind does not topple.

They rise fifteen feet or fifty, tall and straight, three arms lifted high or twenty held in perfect balance. If sun does not scorch, if frost does not wither.

Their roots grow long and shallow, inch by inch, decade to decade, sensing stone as they move, wrapping buried rock to brace them.

They offer their bodies to birds: Harris hawk, Gila woodpecker. Thrasher, flycatcher, elf owl, flicker. A home high in their limbs is safe. A nest inside, dark and cool.

This morning a white-winged dove and red cardinal sat still in a crown of white flowers together, thirty feet above the earth, as if this was their nest, as if by wonder they'd been married.

I heard the great horned owl not yet sleeping, crackle
of crow, coyote answering. The dove spoke softly to her
companion. So sweet and low, her voice fell flower to earth
and rose up through me. The cardinal burned: he spoke in
feather and flame, no need for song: red heart ablaze, red
wings flashing.

Sun struck saguaros high on the ridge. Gold light glowed
through fine needles: every ridge of every pleat, arms and
trunks by spines haloed. Soon petals would begin to fall and
dry and scatter, but tonight flowers would bloom again in
new places, bats would fly, nectar be taken.

3.

Good Samaritan Still Critical. Unconsciously alive, thirty-four hours. Do you dream in flashes of light? In scent, in flower? Do you hear music? Your wife's heart, your daughter's memories?

No wound is too small to kill you. The gilded flicker sometimes digs too deep, severs skeletal rods, leaves the saguaro weak in a thunderstorm. It might survive a torn limb but fall fast to infection that follows.

Sixty years to grow that arm, and this is what happens.

4.

I ask my children to draw something they love or something that scares them. Aisha, Dario, Everett: my students today, misbehaved and misbegotten, born high on crack or addicted to sugar. Adam: locked in a trunk, trapped in a dryer. He has bruises he can't explain: fingerprints on his wrists, rope burns on his ankles. Jamal, Camille, Mikiah: exposed to pesticides and radiation, mercury in the fish, methane in the water. Simone: forgotten in the park one day, befriended by a stranger.

Their teachers bring them to me when they slap themselves or can't stop whirling.

That's Aisha, little dervish, born twelve weeks too soon, shivering and starved, lungs unformed, skin translucent. *I didn't like the air; I wanted to live in water.* She's spun herself sick and now is quiet: Aisha, coloring spotted fish beneath waves of rocking ocean.

Jamal watches the head of a snake rise from paper. Time opens into light, the sensation of heat on Jamal's face where a slant of sun sparks skin and flickers. The hand that draws, the left hand, is warm too, the paper lit, the snake illuminated. Line by line, Jamal moves into the long tranquility of the snake's body. He works on snake time. Very slowly. Jamal Kadir loves each perfect diamond of the Mojave's back, fangs that fold into the mouth, the sound in his throat as he touches the rattle.

They're unpredictable, my children, besieged by dreams, by tics and tremors. They have impulses they can't control, jolts of grief, memories of the future: a world without bats or bees, a planet without flowers.

They love everyone: Saguaro, Hawk, Hummingbird, Tortoise, a Javelina with wings flying over the desert.

Mikiah makes a black hole, a place so dense and dark it warps space and shreds stars. Black is not black enough: he's swirling blue, green, red, purple. *Black holes swallow everything,* he says. *Even light, even color.* He hums as he works, pressing hard on his crayons.

Dario's lost one eye and wears a patch to hide the socket. *An accident?* Yes, but Dario won't say, *a pipe bomb in the street, built and torched by my uncle.* Nine years old and dangerous: Dario Zavala, my beautiful boy, skin pocked and scarred by burning metal.

He'll slash you if you stare. Shoot you if you tease him. He shapes his fingers into guns and kills the children on the playground. Today he's sorry. Today Dario draws a tiny box with bars, the window of a cell, his own small face inside it.

I was afraid, and then I wasn't.

Jamal erases his rattlesnake, touching each line again, leaving the ghost of a snake, hot wind, a wave of light, sand rippling.

Good Samaritan, nobody wants to die. Nothing wants to kill. But sometimes the fuse is lit. Or the snake in its terror bites you.

5.

Lewis Rohe, I whisper your name, husband of Claire, father of Daisi, shot three times by a fourteen-year-old boy: *Juvenile Confesses.*

Dylan McAvee borrowed his mother's car and rolled it down the arroyo. Earlier that day, he snagged her boyfriend's 9mm pistol, wrapped it in a towel, and stashed it under the driver's seat. He didn't have a plan, but he was open to possibilities: Kyle's denim jacket flung on the couch, keys to his truck bulging in the pocket: Kyle and his mother arguing in the bedroom, voices slurred: *Should he save her?* The names of animals, the parts of bodies: *no*: a slap, a kiss, the bedroom door kicked shut: *please*: and then only the sound of the bed hitting the wall over and over: *Mother*:

Plenty of time for a boy to drift into the dizzy heat of day and slip the gun from Kyle's glove box.

Smooth and small, the gun in the hand, surprisingly heavy: he knew the burn in the back of the throat, powder and dirt, the taste after. Just last week, Dylan watched Kyle Truitt shoot a jackrabbit. Such long ears and big feet, beautiful and fast, the rabbit leaping like an antelope, popping high over rocks and cacti, and then the blast: sound itself enough to kill: the rabbit down but not quiet, panting hard, legs twitching, stomach an open wound, dark jumble of bowel spilling. Kyle pressed the gun into his hand, said, *You finish it.*

With eyes on the sides of its head, the jackrabbit sees in all directions.

Kyle Truitt was a poacher, scouting that day for perfect saguaros. He needed the pistol to protect himself from park rangers and Gila monsters. A developer in Sun City paid six hundred cash for every seven-foot saguaro. Transplanted, they'd all die, but very slowly: three years, five: they'd waste and wither.

Forty years to grow that tall, and now no chance to fruit and flower.

Sun seared their heads: not yet noon and both burned, hot and miserable. Kyle had a special order: a fifteen-footer with two arms, *straight, not too many bird holes*. Worth twenty-five hundred, *small bills, day of delivery*. If he found what he needed, he'd come back Monday night with six illegals. *As long as they're here, it's good to employ them.*

He preferred to work with two, but he'd need six to dig fast, to roll a saguaro that size in carpet and hoist it to the truck bed, six small humans to hold it down as they jolted through the desert, tires crushing snake and scorpion, tortoise, tarantula: every living being in their path: cacti, lily, verbena, primrose: every thing unseen, every one unfinished. *I'll need you and your mom, partners at the road, waiting with a U-Haul.*

In his heart, Kyle Truitt hoped for a cristate, a marvelous mutant whose top splayed open into the shape of a fan, a crazy head of curved pleats, a queen, one in one hundred thousand, lovely and strange, ninety-three cristates known to be alive in the whole Sonoran Desert. *In Vegas, she'll go for twenty grand.*

And die in a single year from trauma and travel.

Nothing, no one: three o'clock and fried: the skin of Dylan's arms broke in tiny blisters. The place had been scoured, every seven-footer already gone, a whole generation wiped out by entrepreneurs and rustlers. They found fifteen-footers with stubs, but no two-armed angels.

Kyle started rolling rocks, looking for rattlesnakes. He wanted to shoot again, wanted so much to kill something.

Dylan came home with spines in his hands and legs, barbs in his butt from falling backward. Mother had to pull them out, one by one with tweezers. He hid his face in her pillow, but felt the dark eyes of the jackrabbit watching him from all directions. The saguaros watched too. In morning light, the tall ones on the ridge sensed the man and the boy moving among them. Even now, tonight, the voice of the gun throbbed in their bodies. They raised their arms high and burst with white blossoms. They knew, they remembered. Their long shallow roots heard the rabbit's heart thumping.

Dylan lay exposed on the bed while Kyle walked in and out whenever he wanted, smoked a joint, drank a Corona, finally said, *Come on, Marlene. I'm hungry.*

The saguaros would never forgive him for standing dumb while Kyle emptied nine rounds into one whose single arm had formed in frost and grown downward. *Useless,* he said, as a tiny owl flew from her cool nest deep in the saguaro's body.

Days, months: how long does it take a thirteen-foot cactus to leak its last drop of precious fluid?

Mother smeared cream on his cheeks, then sprinkled him with baby powder. He was a baby: the smell so strong he lost language, so sweet he almost remembered: and the pain was good, delivering him to a time when he was perfectly small and immaculately harmless, to a night when his father lifted him high, and his mother opened her blouse to feed him.

Two hours of twisting spines out, but most were too fine to see, and they prickled even now, seven days later, working their way down, deeper and deeper into him.

Taking the gun, hiding it in Mother's car, was payback for that day of hot grief, a week gone to pain, seven nights of humiliation. Mother pounded on his door. *Going out*, she said. *See you tomorrow*. She reminded him: *forbidden to leave the house for any reason*. When she said that, he thought of fire. Grounded again, circumstantial evidence: forty dollars missing from her purse, two bills peeled off a stack of seven.

Maybe he did, and maybe he didn't. Kyle might have been the one. Mother might have lost or spent them. *No skateboard, no bicycle*. She didn't care about the truth: she was waiting for confession.

14-year-old Boy Shoots Good Samaritan.

Dylan McAvee had been high five days, hopping off the school bus three stops early, slipping down into the canyon. Yes, the spines still stung, slivering their way through flesh and muscle. Only the tremors in his hands and the ache in his jaw distracted him. He couldn't chew; he couldn't swallow. His esophagus burned, some kind of poison: strychnine in the speed, pesticides in the reefer.

The sun set, filling his room with gold light, streaking the sky rose and violet.

He loved the night, the sky on fire. Mother's spare keys waited for him, nested deep in a drawer beneath soft slippery underthings. *Forbidden to touch.* Did she think he didn't know? *These hands have been everywhere.* In the hot cockpit of her car, he unrolled the pistol from the towel and stuffed it in the glove box.

Stars appeared, everything new, anything possible.

All he wanted was some peace from himself, rush of the dark road, windows down, wind blowing. *Jackrabbit, lizard, rattlesnake, saguaro.* If he tossed the gun, would the dead forgive him? *So hungry.* If only he could eat, if only he could swallow. He drank two Red Bulls for the road. *That's the last thing I remember.*

6.

Lewis, you saw a flash of silver in the arroyo, Marlene Ferry's crumpled car upside down, one headlight busted out, one still blindly blazing.

Other drivers had buzzed by, so many, so fast, Dylan McAvee failed to count them. He spun, crazy with pain: the left arm dangled, snapped three times and dislocated at the shoulder. His heart burst in fluttery explosions. He waved the pistol in his right hand, tried to remember how it got there. Now it felt fused to his palm and fingers. Now the little gun, *smooth as soap, chopped and channeled,* ten rounds in the magazine and one more in the chamber, this gun that slayed a jackrabbit and left a saguaro leaking in the desert, this pistol that blasted the head off a rattlesnake and splattered an iguana, had become him: his hand, his arm, his heart, his body.

Saturday Night Shooting Leaves Victim in Coma.

7.

Lewis Rohe, fifty-two years old, father, husband: less than a mile from home, throat raw, joints swollen, muscles depleted by a day filling water tanks in the desert, stiff and sore from gathering garbage tossed by sun-dazed immigrants desperate to lighten their loads as they pushed across the border: you could have blinked hard and not seen.

No one would have known. No one could have blamed you.

You slowed and turned back, called for police and an ambulance. Three minutes, five: no matter how fast they drove, it might not be fast enough.

In the blue beam of your flashlight, you caught the thin shape of a boy spinning in the arroyo, waving one hand, sobbing and swearing.

Stay where you are. I'm coming down for you.

Wounded bird, snared coyote: the child's cries rippled the air, touched your skin and mind, sparked and flared, shimmering through you.

Shush. We're safe now.

You had an emergency kit in the car: saline to flush wounds, duct tape and splints, rolls of gauze, towels to soak blood, compresses to stop it.

The flashlight bounced in your hand, blinding the boy with blue fire. He saw Kyle Truitt scrambling down the wash, a rock in each hand, ready to crush him. Your body blurred, three, not one, the police, he thought, with guns and nightsticks. They'd slam him to the ground, twist the broken arm, cuff his prickling hands behind him.

Cacti everywhere: one more blistering wound, one more fishhook in his face, one more humiliation now would kill him.

You wavered, dark and narrow, a long shadow burning blue: his father back from the war six years ago: Jory McAvee, that horrible halfman, able to walk on a leg and a crutch but sputtering splurred words in some indecipherable language.

Daddy?

Maybe he thought you were God. Maybe he saw a saguaro walking.

Don't be afraid. We'll be okay. I promise.

Words hurt. Too hot, too many. Metal searing his skull, fragments of wire and glass exploding. He aimed for the light. *And I squeezed hard and the gun roared and the gun was me and I squeezed again and again to stop this.*

8.

Home, and the paper still spread on the table tells me the day, the year, the temperature rising, the first four months the hottest on record, *Desierto Peligroso,* ninety-seven immigrants already dead in Arizona desert. The worst still to come: June, July, August. A hundred and ninety-seven more, unknown and unnamed, wandering even now, staggering through Organ Pipe or lost in Cabeza Prieta.

Lewis, do you dream of the disappeared? Are you walking with the dead, leading them to tanks of water? Time and space are one, warping to your weight as you move through them. *Follow me.* Do you hope, do you imagine: water in your mouths, water on your faces. Or have you fallen far behind, even thirstier than they are?

9.

All day, Orlando Cadena measured time by heat and light, the number of thorns piercing flesh: spikes and barbs, needles and nails. The God he thought he knew as one has become many: prickly pear, jumping cholla: catclaws to scratch and tear, a forest of deerhorns to snag and trap him.

The holy cross is not stripped wood, but a living being, slender arms full of spines, body his exact height: *You are the one. Orlando! I make myself in your image.*

What does it mean to refuse God, to stagger past and not embrace him?

Time is water: the last time Orlando and his brother Xavier drank from a plastic bottle, the shame of pissing in pierced hands, the relief of swallowing sweet poison.

So much water wasted! Days ago, or years (who can say? who can remember?), somewhere high in the Quitobaquito Hills, Orlando watched arcs of pale gold catch sun and tremble. God in him. He and his brother laughed, whizzing away their lives, spraying the earth like boys together.

A day's walk, Molina said. *You won't need more than a gallon.*

Nine of them that day, nine plus Molina. Smuggler, thief, liar, pollero: the day three died and two turned back, Jesús Molina pulled a pistol to collect the last eleven gulps of water.

Necessary, he said. *I'll be back with more tomorrow.*

Tomorrow and tomorrow and tomorrow. Molina leaped ahead. Smaller and smaller, he was: coyote, jackrabbit, lizard.

Now thick urine burns its way down, a trickle of steaming sludge, dark as rust, too hot, too foul for Orlando to lift to his split mouth and take back inside him.

Tomorrow. The day after the day Molina disappeared, Guillermo Loma reeled, too sick to stand, eyes scorched red, vessels bursting. Orlando found Molina's shriveled skin, a lizard shrunken in the sand, bones crushed, body flattened, barely the length of Orlando's palm, whip of tail two times longer.

Here is Jesús. Here is your savior. They recognized Molina's empty eyes, wild grin and wasted belly. Guillermo snatched the body fast and tried to eat him.

God swirled up as gold dust, a funnel of light, a flume two hundred feet high, whirling across the blistering desert.

Guillermo heaved and spat blood, and his cousin Martín dropped to his knees to kiss Guillermo's parched mouth, to drink the wine that spilled from him.

The golden God of dust splintered to dark specks against jagged thrusts of lava.

Now they are two, brother and brother. Yesterday, Orlando died. Stumbled into the shade of the mesquite. Felt three-inch thorns stab wrist and shoulder. Xavier had to pull him free. Blood surged from his heart, too thick to fill his wounds, too bitter to wash or heal him.

Rest, here, Xavier said. His face was the face of God, all love, burned skin gone weirdly pale.

Only you. Orlando wanted to speak. *Can only see.* Xavier's open eye, Xavier's raw eyelid. Then he was blind and dead, but he felt his brother's breath, heard his blood moving through them.

While Orlando lay dead in his brother's arms, while Xavier slept or died with him, God shattered himself into a billion sparks, rivers of flickering light, all the light that ever was broken into tiny pieces.

Never, never will it be day again.

Stars pulsed: amber, orange, turquoise, violet. White flares and red implosions. Now, tonight, while the dead watched, whole galaxies popped in and out of existence. Never had Orlando known the names of stars, but he knew them now as he knew their colors. This sphere of broken light was the mind of God, and they were small and dark inside it.

Xavier said, *Walk now.* He meant while we still can. He meant while it's still cool.

They stumbled, tripping over stones, staggering into cacti, crawling toward a new light, the green glow of the horizon. And then, as if by a single thought, the light was whole: God one, God blazing.

When their shadows shriveled and shrank, as sun-seared eyes pulled to slats and dark heads jerked like lizards,

Orlando fell to his knees, scooping sand into his mouth, swallowing hard, trying to drink it.

Xavier whispered, *mañana,* and Orlando wondered if he meant they would die, or be caught, or find water tomorrow.

10.

My brother who does not believe in time does believe in miracles. Leo Derais, thin and white, always the same, ever a child. Forty years now he's been wandering in the desert, walking with the disappeared, the dead, the soon to be taken by birds, the ones burned black who strip from their clothes and swim, cool at last, believing God in his grace turns bajada to water.

He does. He will. My pale brother wavers at the edge of the playa, the shore of a vast lake that once was and now isn't, a bowl of sizzling sand so hot light bends, refracting sky, filling cracked earth with shivery light, the cool blue illusion of water.

Orlando and Xavier are nowhere near this lake, but many times today they've seen sand quiver and shine, God tempting or teaching; and though Xavier learned not to trust the lie, Orlando could not keep his heart from hoping.

Why not believe?

Once every thirty years enough rain falls to fill Willcox Playa with a sheen, a sludge, a soupy mired muck of real water. The eggs of shrimp that have lain dormant for decades hatch in faithful abundance.

Be fruitful and multiply!

If the playa stays wet for two weeks, if the shrimp live, they will do as their bodies command, mate with impetuous joy,

spew eggs in prolific abandon, die as wind blows, shrink as
sun scorches.

Gone again, food for birds, but their patient children sleep
here, eggs in baked clay: thirty, forty, fifty years: surrendering
to sleep, thinking as shrimp think, accepting the miracle.

Good Samaritan, there are ways to measure time that
have nothing to do with being human, ways to survive, to
continue to be, that are not defined by one particular body.

II.

My mother died old at fifty. Nine times we saved and ten times lost her. I hear Chopin's Prélude, A minor, notes played with one hand, *Mother*: first the blot clot in the lung, the lung collapsing: heart attack, stroke, Prélude in D minor, *allegro appassionato*: Coumadin to thin the blood, skin that tears where I touch her, *molto agitato*: nosebleeds we can't stop, blood on the sheets, blood in the shower, *pianissimo*: bruises blooming on her thighs: blue, green, red, purple (Prélude in B flat minor, swallows everything: even light, even color), *precipitando*: diverticula bursting in the bowel, wounds too small to see, *pretissimo*: bacteria spilling into blood, *con brio*:

Mother: septic shock, nocturne for no hands: kidneys clogged, heart failing:

Molto dolce con teneroso: father and daughter alone, submerged beneath an ocean of stars, utterly bedazzled.

Twenty-six years old, and that night I knew I would go home with him, sleep in the bed where I slept as a child, love my father as my own, *till death*, never marry.

Hearts ablaze, bones on fire: who else can ever know? We belonged to each other.

Imagine a song too sweet, vibrations of a black hole whirling in space, shredding stars that come too close, humming through time (swallowing light, swallowing color), tuned to B flat, fifty-seven octaves too low for any human being to hear it: imagine: nine billion years of sound, and only stars listening.

12.

Good Samaritan! Just today, Simone saw a javelina with wings flying over the desert. Tonight, alone in his room, locked in his closet, bare bulb buzzing above his head, Everett is making the eye of a bee, all sixty-nine hundred lenses.

He's divided his paper into tiny squares, four thousand and eight so far: he'll need another sheet tomorrow. For now, he wants to shade each lens on this page a different color. *To see what the bee sees, inside the flower.*

When he's done with the eye, he'll give it to Dario.

13.

Yes, it's true, the bees are vanishing, not just dying, but disappearing, buzzing away from the hive at dawn and not returning.

Their bodies are perfect:

On the seventh day, God did not rest: God began to imagine the honeybee and the flower. Time blossomed into light, the infinite possibilities of perception. One hundred million years of thought, and even now the evolution of love continues.

Our strange sister!

Who but God can fathom: two compound eyes, each with sixty-nine hundred lenses, four filigree wings beating two hundred thirty times per second:

Behold the honeybee!

Thirteen millimeters long, ninety-nine milligrams:

I make myself in her image.

As she flies, foraging for nectar and pollen, the friction of wind through feathery hairs builds a static charge, her body electric.

Above or below, the flower opens: infinite blue, worlds of yellow, a murmuration of white shimmering into thirteen thousand eight hundred lenses.

She's blind to red, but sees a universe we can't know, galaxies beyond violet.

So lovingly she lands!

Pollen jumps into the hairs of her charged body. Hidden in the flower's folds, she plunges the tube of her proboscis deep, flicks her long tongue, sips love's holy nectar.

She can drink herself drunk and buzz away dizzy. Each time she rises, her body glows, dusted with pollen. All day she moves, transferring life one flower to another, fertilizing ovaries that swell to ripened fruit and feed the world: five thousand blossoms in a day: a hundred and seventy-five thousand in her lifetime: forty days:

Until her wings wear thin, until her tattered body falls and fails.

She pollinates apples, pears, pecans, strawberries: avocados, almonds, squash, kiwis: oranges, peaches, soybeans, cherries: papaya, pepper, mango, coffee: blueberries, grapefruit, cantaloupe, broccoli: lemons, limes, clover, celery:

Behold the honeybee who makes your life possible.

She is the spark between: without her, they cease to be, and we soon shall follow.

Imagine pollinating your own blossoms, scrubbing anthers, gathering pollen, carrying your treasure home in tiny baskets, remembering to dry it for two days at precisely the right temperature, returning to your fields and orchards, lying on your belly in the dirt or climbing high to fertilize each flower. You carry a tiny duster made of bamboo and chicken feathers. Too much is too much. One light dip, one flick, one flutter: *may you dwell in the open heart*: clear your mind of all distraction.

Good Samaritan, as we lose our lives, we will love this world. Here is the path to peace, kneeling on the earth, bowing to the flower, surrendering our will blossom by blossom.

14.

My brother who does not believe in time, remembers the future: 72 *Migrants Slain*. One survives to tell the story. One walks thirteen miles, pressing his hand hard against the wound in his neck. One eighteen-year-old man, protector and guardian of eight siblings, a pregnant wife, a grandmother in Ecuador: one boy who traveled two months and paid a smuggler fifteen thousand dollars to guide him to America: one who hoped to earn enough to keep his people alive, to feed them: this one heard all the others die ninety miles from the border.

We refused to carry drugs, and so Los Zetas shot us.
(One boy falls beneath the body of another.)

We came from Honduras, Brazil, Guatemala, El Salvador.
(So easily the body opens!)

We died with our hands bound.
(So easily becomes blood and bowels, legs twitching.)

We died with dirty rags as blindfolds.

15.

Butterfly, bee, bat, saguaro: hummingbird, moth, ant, ocotillo: javelina, hawk, rattlesnake, vulture: scorpion, bear, bighorn, quail: dove, owl, woodpecker, thrasher: tortoise, gecko, warbler, raven: iguana, whiptail, perch, cicada: cardinal, pine, cypress, juniper: willow, poppy, grackle, iris: yarrow, primrose, tree frog, sunflower: catfish, columbine, salsify, verbena: flax, gentian, tanager, lupine:

On the seventh day, God in His rapture said:

I make you all as one in my image!

Today, just today, Simone saw a bear adrift in turquoise water, golden fur, tinted auburn.

Problem Bear Caught Swimming in Tucson Pool.

She's been relocated three times: sprayed with a fire extinguisher, stunned with tranquilizers: *sleep is death, so thirsty:*

She's awakened dry and dizzy, unknown, a stranger to herself, abandoned in another country.

No map, no compass: the golden bear has walked sixty miles in six days, navigating by stars, the taste of pine whirling in wind, aspen quivering high, the flight of hawks, the sound of woodpeckers: the names of mountains mean nothing to her: she smells a bear she knows, skunks and deer, a family of crows, one particular mountain lion: she hears the river roaring full, knows as home the scent of tannin:

Now she's stunned again and sinking fast: snared by a net of grief: falling into death: breathing blue water.

At the mission one day I saw fifty barefoot boys all carrying crosses: hot sand, sun blistering: they walked on burned feet: crowns of thorns stabbed their foreheads:

To know our savior's pain: to bear his burden:

Lewis:

It is the body, not the mind, that teaches us compassion: swollen brain, fractured femur, the weight of my sister against my hip, the wheeze and gasp of your father breathing.

16.

Sound is touch, waves of vibrating air, black holes and bees, vibrations traveling through time, your wife's voice box compressing air, *Lewis*: and now those trembling waves enter the channel of your ear, touch your eardrum: her voice not yet a voice touches hammer, anvil, stirrup, the tiniest bones of all the bones inside your wounded body: *Lewis*: sound is touch: waves splashing in a secret sea, whirling deep into the coil of the cochlea where vibrations shiver through fine hairs, your perfect, holy, unseen cilia: *sound is touch*: charging molecules: *Lewis*: sparks of electricity form a pattern in your brain: words, love, your wife's voice: if only you could make sense, if only you could answer:

Lewis:

17.

All day you measured time by gallons of water. You knew nothing of the night to come, the silver car, the boy, the arroyo.

Your route took you deep into Cabeza Prieta, to three emergency drinking stations where brilliant blue polyethylene drums sat cradled in steel frames, waiting for you to flush and fill, to purify with drops of chlorine.

A blue flag on a 30-foot pole flapped in hot wind to mark each station.

Most of the drums are recycled syrup barrels, donated by *Coca-Cola* because nobody, legal or illegal: nobody: white, brown, kind, or stupid deserves to die of thirst trying to cross the Sonoran Desert.

You've found the bodies, the ones left behind, skin mummified to hard leather, eyes pecked out, flesh so parched and poisoned even the birds refuse to open them.

They fell two miles or two hundred feet from water. You've held smooth bones: vertebrae of a snake, skull of a rabbit. You've touched the dead: brother, father, sister, child.

At the first station, you found two drums riddled with holes, shot and stabbed, spigots pulled out and stolen, the word *AGUA* slashed with red paint, replaced with other words that wound and kill you.

Three dead quail hung upside down, dangling from the steel frame, feet tied with fine wire. Who needs words to read this message? You untied the birds. Living, each weighed six ounces, and its wings spanned fourteen inches. Mostly, the quail preferred to walk or run. You don't know why, but you love to see them flee on foot, black plumes at the tops of their heads bobbing.

In early morning, as they drift down from trees where they've spent the night drowsing, their sad, whoopeling voices burble up and out of them like cool water.

Dead and dehydrated, the birds weighed less than breath, wind and sand, hot dust choking you.

You and three other volunteers replaced the drums, unspooled the long hose from the water tank in your truck, and set the gas pump humming.

Any night, the vandals might return to slash or shoot, stab or poison. *Blue is good.* Any day, vigilantes might wait here, disguised as immigrants, tie you to a tree while they blast holes through the tank on the truck, puncture your radiator, nail your tires. *Blue means water.*

Vengeance is slow. Thirst has no mercy. The water they spill could save four hundred.

Traitor: you aid and abet, you comfort the enemy.

Every Saturday for five years you've come to the desert to sustain the dark horde, the ones who risk their lives for the privilege of slaughtering cows or plucking chickens, the alien invaders, willing to work twelve-hour days splattered with blood, slicing their hands, losing their fingers, the dangerous swarm, surging across the border, hundreds and thousands, ready to die, but hoping to pick oranges, pecans, strawberries, avocados, grateful to prune trees or wash windows, singing as they get down on their knees to scrub floors, scour toilets, prepared to paint your house, relieved to mow the golf course.

They look just like you inside: ribs, spines, femurs, clavicles. Their bones are small, but arranged exactly the same way, in precisely the same numbers.

At each station, you found trash and treasure: cans with their tops punched open, a knife with a broken blade, a bible, a hymnal, a woman's shoe with a three-inch heel, razors, rosary beads, a bicycle with flat tires. You found a white dove, carved from two pieces of wood, one for the wings, one for the body, sweatshirts trampled in dust, prayer cards, a baby stroller.

All too heavy to take, all too much to carry.

You and your companions filled five black bags with garbage.

18.

The honeybee flies three miles and returns to the hive to dance for her sisters, body abuzz, wings humming: a spin, a turn, tones rising and falling: in this way, she tells them where and how far and which direction to go to find the sweet well of holy nectar. Charged body singing with sound, she is their memory of the future: her dance in the present, in the eternal *now* of her existence, unveils the past and foretells a journey.

If she's sick, afflicted with viruses and fungi, unable to digest pollen, if she's dazed, high on the toxins in pesticides, she won't return: she'll die alone to save the others.

I see my brother's pale body covered with bees. They're doing their dance for him, buzzing and turning. He's not afraid. He knows where they go when they disappear. He's learning their language.

Be quick, I say. *We won't live long without them.*

19.

Sound is touch: home, alone in your bed, the new day just beginning, Claire presses your cell phone to her ear, hears you whispering, *Noemí, Nazario, their baby Idalia, Oaxaqueños,* voice notes to yourself, *Zapotecs we met at the third station.*

You washed and bandaged Noemí's feet. *Bruised and blistered, too swollen to fit in her shoes. Water hurt, bones broken.* You pulled spines from their hands. Each wound flared, hot with infection. *We gave them antibiotic ointment, moleskin, lip balm.*

You tried to persuade Nazario to let you transport them to a hospital, but *no, por favor—no, gracias.*

We gave them applesauce and mandarin oranges, tuna, Spam, salted peanuts.

Idalia was still flushed and fat, thriving on her mother's milk, *but yesterday the milk stopped coming.*

We gave them formula and a bottle, diaper wipes and six diapers. You tried again. *Your wife can't walk. Please, for the baby.*

Very softly Nazario whispered, *Si, por Idalia.* He meant there was nothing for her on the other side. *Suerte o muerte,* luck or death. He meant they weren't going back there.

20.

The bears are dangerous, it's true: armed with teeth and claws, the will to stun, the patience to eat you: *so hungry*: following trails of trash: *losing their fear*: killing the dog, gulping down dog food: *habituating to humans*: guzzling our milk, shredding our couches: *evolving three hundred times too fast*: pounding on doors, bashing through windows:

We've stolen their land, diverted their water: scorched their earth with drought and fire: starved their cubs: paved their canyons:

We've planted our seed:

peach, pear, pecan, apple:

Now they're tearing down limbs to feast in our orchard.

21.

In the dark dark, I dance in my sleep. Mother plays a tender waltz, *Gymnopédies,* fingers light as breath, barely touching keys.

Later, she transfigures the night: E flat minor, D major: inharmonic change, that weird frisson: *sound is touch*: in the space between notes, the bones sing, aching to hear lost music.

My brother kneels in the back of the Chrysler, understanding at last how time moves at different speeds in both directions. He's trembling now, but can't speak. *Time does not exist. Time is perception.*

Here is the night: cobalt sky, violet desert: my father's eyes almost closed: no, we don't stop: *no, I'm not tired*: the car veering into the left lane: *there's no reason why we can't remember the future*: lights of a truck heading north: holding us in this moment:

A horn pitched to A sharp: into the night still blaring:

Mother plays with one hand because the right hand is crushed, the right arm is splintered: *Mother*: because she held Joelle tight in her left arm, and used her right arm to brace them.

Skull of a desert fox, bones of a missing child:

There is a place I can go on that road, a line I can draw on a map: a frontier, a border: my country before, my country after: *Joelle:*

Just today, just this morning, the song of you, a wave of sound, a coyote across the arroyo howling.

The coroner found charred bones under the car. Little tortoise, quick rabbit: she could have been anyone: a bird or a bat, a javelina with wings: there was so little left of her.

No one told me where. I don't know how I know this.

(This part is true, this I remember: tiny slivers of glass working their way out of our flesh for months after: glass in our arms, glass in our faces, spots of blood on our clothes, no one asking.)

22.

The first bullet shattered your clavicle, burned a hole, traveling upward, exploded out your back, and still you clung to the light, and still you stumbled forward. The second, third, and fourth whizzed past your face. Even now, tonight, the voice of the gun speaks through bone and muscle, throbs in the skull, jolts with each heartbeat. The fifth bullet caught your hand; the sixth blasted rocks behind you. The seventh found your thigh, and this one finally stopped you.

Lewis:

You dropped to your knees and folded backward. *Whoosh of blood, breath, whisper*: you heard the voices of people in cars.

Pain surprised, because not unbearable.

Burned flesh, bullets tearing: you smelled sweet smoke, copper and dust, your father's closet: remembered standing in the close dark: sweat and dirt: limp arms, shirts dangling.

Nine years old you were, your father dead of silicosis: lungs hard as glass, each cell a prism: crystalline dust of the mine: dust deep in the body.

You did not expect to survive.

How far can you walk? How much can you carry?

Leather and bone: your father barely a hundred pounds:

But so hard to lift, so weirdly heavy.

Already your heart beat too fast.

The body ten percent human cells, sixty-two percent water.

You wanted to touch your wounds, press hard, *breathe*, try to stand, try to stay here, but your hands lay limp at your sides, tingling arms too weak to lift them.

So little to call your self.

Bats flew high.

So thirsty!

You wanted to drink with them, one last time, sweet nectar.

A woman weeping, a man muttering.

You lay with your father in the dark, heard your mother and him for each breath gasping.

Whoosh of blood, breath, whisper:

You felt the universe expand, the space inside bone, the space between atoms:

Lewis:

There is a sound inside all other sound, a place where the song is whole, where you are safe inside your mother. Hers was the first voice, yours the first music playing: rivers of blood, breath rushing: the sweet syncopation of your hearts, the rhythm of love, soft or racing:

Lewis:

Now this sky, this earth, stones and stars, black holes whirling in space: space opening now: the space between cells, the space between galaxies:

Now: the light of stars long dead, surge of blood, lungs heaving:

Lewis:

Your heart fluttering too fast:

Now:

A siren:

Your body flung in the sand, the voices of bats above you.

Now:

White flowers of the saguaro opening wide as your open hands to tempt them:

And now, even now: somewhere far away, the boy you hoped to love can't stop wailing.

23.

My children are famous: lost, stolen, accused, convicted: *Eight-year-old Boy Sells Handgun to Classmate*: I see their faces on the news, read their names in the paper: *Battered Baby Found Alive in Motel Room*. They crash their bikes into walls, fly off bridges on their skateboards. Simone leaps from her mother's car and cracks her skull on the pavement. They disappear in the park, return as bones in the desert. *Two Toddlers Perish in Trailer Fire*. One survives: that's Camille. *Home alone*, she says. *If I'd been awake, I could have saved them*. Five years old that night, and now she's seven. She remembers the sticky taste of cough syrup, *to help you sleep, my love*, a cool hand on her face, the smell of beer, a smear of lipstick, Mother kissing her goodnight: *Close your eyes, be a good girl*.

Twin Boys Accused of Arson.

Lewis: how can you lie so still? How can you be so quiet?

Today, Camille stands at the window, paper taped to the glass, breathing three hummingbirds to life as light flashes through them. She clutches a fistful of crayons. Wings blur blue and green. Throats shimmer rose and violet.

Three invisible hearts beat twelve hundred times per minute.

If I'd been awake, I could have saved us.

Mikiah discovers the radiant end of a star's life, gas glowing in space, remnants of a supernova. A star fifty million light years gone, and just now touching us.

My beautiful children! Hovering between time and death, in this moment haloed.

Lewis, I confess: the boy who shot you could be one of mine: Aisha, Dario: any child I love: *Problem Bear Rips Roof off Motor Home in Santa Ritas:*

So hungry!

Dylan McAvee crouches in the corner of his cell, waiting for you to die and destroy or wake and save him.

Three Problem Bears Euthanized in Huachuca Mountains. They look just like us inside. Just like us, skinned naked.

No shoes, no belt, no crayons, no paper: the boy's on suicide watch but has found a way, is weaving a rope with threads pulled from his mattress.

Problem Bear Kills Three Goats in Sierra Vista.

Who can explain a child's weird luck, bullets that might have so easily missed, somehow instead miraculously found you.

So human the cries of a goat: so long to die: so late we heard them.

Mikiah, Adam: armed with grief, lit by terror: *any child I love*: a memory of home, a canyon, a mother: Simone, Camille: delirious with pain: Jamal, Aisha: a scatter of buckshot wounds gone septic:

Lewis:

That bear took five bullets in the brain before he stopped, before he staggered:

Nine pints of blood lost and still leaking.

Dylan McAvee remembers the jackrabbit's wild eye and open body, its ridiculously huge ears, the vibration of his own heart, the blast of the gun through bone hammering.

The shadows of birds pass, a flicker of peace, but no refuge.

Now Everett is at the window too, finishing the eye of the bee, his gift for Dario. Light fills each luminous lens. In an exaltation of white, the eye sees its own beauty.

24.

I hear Chopin played with both hands: *andantino, lento, agitato, vivace*: so lightly Mother moves one prélude to another: *allegro appassionato*: my body in hers, my unborn children in me: every egg already formed: everything, everywhere, to be and not to be, the endless rearrangement of sound, within Chopin's Préludes present.

Lewis:

25.

You think if no one touches you, you will die: but you need not fear: they are always touching: adjusting tubes and needles, speaking softly: the one who calls himself Olumide bathes you with a soft rag: *sound is touch*: sings to you in his language.

The space between cells, the space between galaxies: Olumide: a wave of sound inside a stone, breath moving between bodies.

There are memories that won't form: your father not dead: your mother before blind, before snakes invaded the house, before terrified, before dementia: *Mother*: your sister unborn, but in the womb with you.

Skull of a desert fox, bones of a missing child: my country before, my country after:

Last summer your Daisi disappeared, and now, today, as light touches your face, as webs of gold light break across your broken body, as waves shatter to sparks through closed eyelids: now, today, as light, you dream her.

She's only ten, but if you sleep too long, your little girl will get away from you. She has a secret life, a pink purse stuffed in the back of her closet, a yellow dress with red flowers, years too small to wear, and anyway, she wouldn't. She's clipped her hair short and wears low-slung jeans to school. You glimpse a scorpion at the base of her spine, a temporary tattoo that one day soon a tattooed man will needle into her.

Birds flutter out of your broken heart: *Daisi!*

You remember carrying the pink purse when she was too tired, Daisi dancing in her yellow dress, Daisi blurred with brilliant poppies. Only at the edge of sleep does she forget and call you *Daddy*.

Last August she rode her bicycle around the block while you repaired the gutter torn free by rain and left dangling. *Three blocks*, you said. *No more in any direction.*

What do limits mean to a girl like Daisi?

Alone all day: Claire at work noon to midnight: your wife pacing the halls of the hospital where she falls in love with babies wounded in the womb: *shivering and starved*: a girl with a hole in her heart, a two-pound boy born to his mother in prison.

Daisi circled again and again, the bike metallic blue, her short dark hair by wind ruffled. *Is this all you know?* She rang her little bell, or glided by without you catching her.

Twelve minutes, twenty: hot in the sun, teetering on the ladder: how long did you work before you realized Daisi was glinting and gone, a whole hour vanished?

You found the sparkling bike abandoned under the bridge, Daisi somewhere down the wash, clouds swollen with rain rolling toward you.

Soon this river of sand would roar cold full of water.

Vertebrae of a deer, shell of a tortoise: you've touched the dead: you know how it can be: *Daisi!* You wailed her name into the wind, saw your whole life lost in this moment, years of grief, white-winged doves in dark sky, a hundred birds suddenly rising.

You ran down the wash. *When it fills, I'll catch you.*

Then she was there, waving from the bridge, calling you back, Daisi saving you. Sun slanted through clouds, and in this light, everything you believed shimmered and vanished.

Lightning now and rain, the sky dark as dusk, the wash full and roiling. You and Daisi huddled under the bridge, whelmed by a torrent of sound that spared you from speaking.

Then it was day again, the rain barely a drizzle, the sky opening into blue, each molecule of air a prism: turquoise, gold, orange, violet. Daisi rode ahead, and you walked home alone in the rain, and only the rain touched you.

Never never did you tell Claire the truth of it. You want to weep now and confess: lie upon lie, each one a wound that to this day pierces you. By the time Claire returned, the bike was clean, your clothes washed and warm, spun dry and folded. Why tell her now? Why make her worry? The torn gutter flapped free, and you said, *The storm came before I finished.*

You lay in your bed, eyes wide, heart stammering: *Daisi.* Only she can know you now, only Daisi bears your secret.

You walked down the hall and she was there, awake like you, but pretending not to be.

26.

Good Samaritan, no wound is too small to kill you. Twenty-two years my father and I lived alone without my mother. Imagine a day like this one: ocotillos fifteen feet high, clusters of long stems, tips inflamed with red flowers: iridescent birds flashing in and out, the smallest on earth, hummingbirds hovering in space, stealing nectar: *till death do us part*: imagine: a row of palo verde trees, green skin, yellow blossoms: prickly pear bursting into bloom: piercing light, my father driving home: thirty scarlet hearts, the claret cup breaking open.

Twenty-two years and then one day, no more, imagine:

Light stabs his eyes, radiates down his spine, sparking nerves: finger, femur, lip, pelvis: thorns of light: pain so precise he sees an image of himself, a path inside, nerves illuminated.

The creosote blooms ten thousand years, casting clones of itself in all directions. Roots of the Joshua tree tap dry earth, sensing water. Nine hundred years old and still it grows down in the dark and up to the light, lifting leaves eight inches long, thin and stiff and sharp as daggers.

The light, the birds, feathers shattering light, wings igniting: this is the hurt: their hearts in him, a wild fluttering. If he can just swerve to the side of the road, breathe, wipe the cold sweat from his face, cover his eyes with a rag, stop this light, turn down the air-conditioning.

Lewis, my father's wound is a tiny tear deep in the inner wall
of the aorta where blood begins to spill, to pool and press,
to rip as it weakens the vessel wall, to pulse, to surge, to
rupture.

(Thirty scarlet hearts, the claret cup breaking open.)

So hard to pull the wheel with one hand: the left arm throbs
and goes numb and the hand lies limp in his lap and why
can't he use it?

Barb of the jumping cholla, thorn of the mesquite, leaf of
the Joshua shooting through him. He does not know, cannot
imagine where or what or why so sudden.

He wants to stomp the brake and be done, but the right
leg goes weak, the body remembers: bones broken long ago
lined now with cracks and fissures. The car rumbles along
the shoulder, skids and jolts and finally shivers.

Good Samaritan, you can bleed to death with no blood
leaking out of you. Die on the side of the road hours before
your daughter imagines: ocotillo in flames, palo verde in
blossom.

Here is the face of love: three children who tap on the glass,
who pound, who kick hard, who hammer, who speak no
English, who break the passenger window with a rock, who
unlock the door and climb inside, who cut bare knees, who
cut small fingers, who touch my father's face, who forget
their Spanish, who speak in trill, in ripple and murmur,
whose voices are love, birdsong and water.

The disappeared leave their blood in my father's car. I read their signs. I hear their voices: dove, quail, warbler:

The cactus wren flies in and out of her nest between fishhooks and barbs, needles and nails, flits unharmed through spines of the cholla.

Nothing snags. Nothing hurts her.

Twilight: I stand at the side of the road, touch the cool green skin of palo verde, begin to count the blossoms on a single branch, trying to believe it.

27.

Just today pink petals floated in a looping line across the sidewalk. A mystery lovely and strange: hundreds of black ants, each one hoisting a torn blossom.

Imagine their impossible strength, the beauty of a single mind moving between many bodies.

Were they drunk with sweet scent, besotted by wilted flowers?

Down a slope of sand through catclaw and cholla, I followed to find a dome of pink light, the ants covering their little hill, a cathedral of trembling petals.

So moist and cool inside!

Safe from the sun they were, blessed and protected. Who among them was the first to trip upon the gift and perceive its wonder? Which one of ten thousand left a perfect trail of pheromones: a prayer, a poem, a promise: we might live another day, restored by torn flowers.

Three hundred and sixty-nine days gone, my father is, and still I ran home to tell, to bring him back, to show him.

Good Samaritan, I am telling you. I have fallen in love with you. I am whispering in your sleep. *Sound is touch.* Keep faith in our survival.

28.

Why do you call me good? Everything is good: me, you, the boy waving the gun: I hear him now, crying in the arroyo: I saw the car rolled and tried to help, but the boy with the gun was afraid and fired: the rattlesnake is good, the saguaro, the rabbit: the blood of strangers sings in my veins: they know not what they do: I hear the voices of multitudes: lava, gneiss, quartz, granite: sand that becomes stone that becomes sand: all that is through time: a song vibrating in bone long after notes vanish: vertebrae, fibula, clavicle, sacrum: black holes humming in space, fourteen billion years of sound, a universe of song, all that is, before and after: the gray fox climbs trees, the bighorn sheep sees two miles: who among us is not good: what being not holy: scorpion, wasp, catclaw, cholla: the vulture finds the dead and purifies the world: poppy, lupine, iris, lily: who do you not love: what being is unworthy? The problem bear is good: she walks with me across the desert: the agave fruits once and dies, its seed exploding in the world: heart, hand, eye, pelvis: which part do you not need: thunder, rain, river, lightning: who here is not perfect: at dusk, white-winged doves circle, looking for water, a reflection of sky on earth: blue is good, so good: God, a fallen cloud: we have never been this thirsty.

29.

Nazario has made a sling of his shirt to carry Idalia. His back burns, cracks and blisters. The distance between life and death is forty-two ounces, warm water slapping a plastic jug, its weight tugging his arm, temptation his heavy reminder.

He won't drink. Every ounce is for Idalia. He flicks drops on her hot skin to calm and cool her. When he squats to rest, he fills her bottle one swallow at a time. *Here is your mother.*

He speaks now only Zapoteco, the dialect of his village high in the Sierra de Madre de Oaxaca, the language of his wife, the songs of his mother. Why insist on Spanish here? Why teach Idalia broken English? His grandmother begged him not to go. *I am old and forgetting.* He whispers to Idalia in Macaria's tongue. *You will be our memory.*

Every few steps, he drops a tiny scrap of colored paper, trash he's found and resurrected: a prayer, a poem, a map, a story, a path that leads home to his wife Noemí.

She is far behind or far ahead of them. They left her in the scattered shade of a mesquite. No word, no kiss, no baby's cry could wake her.

Sleep, my love. Let sleep heal you.

Now, in late afternoon, a blacktail rattlesnake flows into the shade and coils beside her. He has no wish to harm or strike, no need to warn or rattle.

In his fifteen-year life he's struck twenty-one times: woodrat, flicker, cottontail, gecko. Together these strikes equal less than one minute, bright flares illuminating ecstasies of time. After he swallowed the bird, he lay still for nine days, digesting. He can survive a year without food, seasons without water. Each day opens into the bliss of heat and light, the poetry of pure sensation.

He knows the animal beside him by her taste in the air, a scent he catches with one flick of his forked tongue, one tender touch to holes on the roof of his mouth, openings to the organ inside where taste becomes human.

He hears her heart: a stuttering vibration amplified by earth, her body to his, muscle to vertebrae. The footfalls of mice, the skitterings of lizards, the rasp of wrens, the whoops of quail come as voices in his own skull: he has no ears, no holes outside his head to open.

The wild human pulse shimmers up his spine, jitters his jaw, sets the delicate bones of his inner ears quivering.

He sees inside her body, perceives her as warm waves wafting into pits on his face, opening ion channels, triggering nerves to the optic tectum where vision refines heat to form a shivery field of radiant colors, an infrared thermal image: gold and orange, rimmed with turquoise.

A flame inside a flame: if he wanted to kill, he sees where to strike her. The core blazes red. The human heart hammers.

Noemí, Noemí, Noemí.

The water is hot now. Nazario takes one long pull and then another. He can't stop himself. Water spills on his face, spatters to hot sand, vanishes as vapor.

Idalia does not move. Idalia does not whimper. He drops the empty jug. One less burden to carry. The last ounce fills his mouth. He can spit it in Idalia's mouth or close burned eyes and swallow.

Noemí. He would weep now if he could, but his tears are salt inside him. He kneels down to cradle the child, to taste her hot breath, no longer sweet, no longer milky. He spits the water between Idalia's cracked lips, feels the warm stream, luck or death, pass between them.

When he tries to stand, he discovers his hips and knees have locked; his cramped muscles will not lift him. Now he must crawl or die, fall down on Idalia or try to carry her. She swings heavy in the shadow of his body. There is no one else on earth to love. Thorns pierce his palms. Sand burns his fingers. Three feet or thirty. They might live another day. They might meet another creature.

Through closed eyelids, Noemí sees the shadows of birds descending, two then five then twenty, bodies dark and beautiful, rocking in air, not flapping, wings catching light, feathers sparking silver, the shadow of one wide enough to hold her whole body: *Noemí*.

The snake uncoils and flows into the desert. He ripples when he moves, sinuous spine composed of two hundred eighty-four vertebrae, a pair of ribs for each one, thousands of elegant muscles to move them. As an embryo, a snake inside a snake, his secret self formed tiny bones that might have become legs, but didn't. So much easier to flex, to flow, to move side to side, to slide on sand without them.

Noemí Amaya offers her body to birds: they have come to shield her from the sun: God has sent them here to save her.

30.

Illegal Immigrant Deaths Spiral to New Highs in Arizona:
so many dead the Pima County Medical Examiner uses a refrigerated truck to hold them: three or four to a slot: little tortoise, quick rabbit: they could be anyone: a bird or a bat, a javelina with wings:

There is so little left of them:

My brother walks bone to bone, body to body. *Desierto Peligroso*. June, July, August: the worst still to come: a day in December when he will find the fragile skeleton of a child nested in the ribcage of her father:

But now, today, Nazario Amaya hears the voices of birds, the skitterings of lizards:

Now:

Nazario hears breath, blood: his child's fluttering heart: the claret cup breaking open:

Lewis:

Olumide is speaking your name, has come to bathe you, to touch with warm hands, to wash with warm water: his voice swirls deep in the coil of the cochlea: you begin to hum with him, to speak with him, to buzz with sound, to be, to answer: *poppy, lupine, iris, lily*: the air inside and outside trembles: *everything is good*: Olumide lifts one limp leg and then the other: washes between, is not afraid of you: *the rattlesnake is good, the saguaro, the rabbit*: the blood of strangers sings in your veins: *who do you not love: what being is unworthy*: waves of sound touch your eardrums: *sand that becomes stone that becomes sand: all that is through time: a song vibrating in bone even now as notes vanish*: the air dries your legs fast: Olumide is washing your stomach, your buttocks: *lava, gneiss, quartz, granite*: Olumide is washing your feet: *vertebrae, fibula, clavicle, sacrum*: a sudden surge of sound: *thunder, rain, river, lightning*: a spark, a tremor: Olumide presses hard on your soles, and with both feet you kick him:

Lewis!

He is laughing now, and something like a bark bursts out of you:

Is good? he says.

Yes, is.

Yes, perfect.

He leans close to your ear, whispers words in his language, washes your face again, touches your eyelids.

Lewis: sparks of electricity form a pattern in your brain: words, love, Olumide's voice: *Shush, it's okay*: the light is touching your face, your hand, your thigh, your naked feet: *Shush, sir, it's okay*: his voice touches your unseen cilia:

: :

You're alone with him, alive, weeping.

31.

Last night Orlando Cadena died for the second time, fell to his knees in a dry wash, digging fast, smelling water. So close! He lay flat on the earth, pressing his face into the hole, opening his mouth to receive: but no, not here, nothing: the sand damp for an instant, then dry again as air touched it.

He rolled to his back, flung his arms wide, called to his brother on the shore: *Xavier, I'm floating!*

Stars pierced his chest, and the scorpion he caught under his knee whipped her barbed tail fast and stung him.

The God of sound entered: wasp, bee, cricket, cicada: skittering under skin: chirp, scratch, hum, chitter: a stridulation of song buzzing bone and blood, quivering heart and liver: *now you know*: nothing but sound, everywhere, all of him.

The heart kicked hard, out of rhythm: *Orlando*: the body twitched in the sand, heaved and spasmed, back arching so hard Xavier Cadena heard his brother's spine crackling.

Now the sounds inside are the voices of multitudes, the disappeared, the dead, wandering in the desert. They've fled Nicaragua and Belize, Guatemala and Ecuador: Jalisco, Michoacán, Oaxaca, Chiapas: surged from Colombia, Colima, Hildago, Guerrero: they've run for their lives: escaped Veracruz and Honduras, Sinoloa, El Salvador. The Hohokam and Anasazi are here, still looking for water.

Wind pushes them across cracked earth. Some have lost their arms or legs, some their hearts or faces. In the blaze of a new day Orlando Cadena rises from his river of sand to walk among them.

They speak their native tongues, ten thousand words for water.

Dark birds offer the temptation of wings, shade and refuge. *Fall to your knees, Orlando! Fall to your face again, and we will come down for you.*

Mother said, *From El Mozote and La Joya, Cerro Pando and Los Toriles, the birds took everything: cows, dogs, chickens, my sisters: goats, pigs, horses, my father: they took my mother and brother but not me: blood and dirt and bone: I crawled on my belly: I lay mouth down in the dirt: I was dead: I was nothing.*

Adelina Luna, Orlando's mother, yes, one day, she will be, but that day, the last day of her life as a child, Adelina Luna, six years old, did not imagine two sons, three daughters, believed only what she saw: streets of blood, the world on fire.

Go, her mother said. *You will be our witness.*

The Salvadoran soldiers scorched the mountains of Morazán with M16's and 90mm recoilless rifles, M60 machine guns and 81mm mortars: gifts from their benefactors in America, and by American soldiers trained to use them. Still they preferred to crush skulls with rocks and slash throats with machetes. Still they hung children from trees or flung them high in the air to snag on their bayonets. Still they torched the towns:

As if fire could hide us.

Clavicle, jaw, sternum, patella: pelvis, sacrum, femur, fibula: metatarsal, skull, rib, vertebrae:

You can't hide the dead. One by one the birds rose heavy with our flesh, and light touching bone illuminated how we died here.

Orlando!

All these years, the seventeen long years of his life, Orlando Cadena has failed to understand his mother's story. Now he sees what she saw: the bones of a fetus cradled in the pelvis of her mother: now he hears girls crying in the hills, entered again and again because the soldiers preferred the weapons of their bodies: he hears the child who sang, who wouldn't stop no matter what they did to her: she praised God as they shot her in the chest, sang to her sisters as blood flowed in rivers out of her: she sang to God her father as five more soldiers entered: and now they were afraid, and now they slashed and stabbed, and finally she lay still, and finally she lay quiet.

Orlando hears her high, clear voice rippling down dark mountains, proof that God is here, alive, the girl inside him: sound is touch: the girl's voice touching him.

I lived for her, his mother said. *Because she sang until she died, because she wanted me to tell you.*

Yes, Orlando: the heart breaks and breaks open: the world falls inside as the God of pain enters.

At dusk God appears as a saguaro with thirteen arms, eleven raised up high, two formed in frost growing downward: a tiny owl flies out of the saguaro's body, proof that the soul has weight, wings and breath, eyes that see everywhere. She catches a scorpion and removes its stinger, swallows it down and rises up chattering.

Orlando! What is your mind if not this sky streaked coral and rose, magenta and turquoise? What is a thought if not this bird flying through you? Where is God if not right here, body bursting into bloom, arms opening wide, breaking into white blossoms?

And Xavier is saying, *Welcome back, little brother,* and the night has come again, and the light into stars has shattered.

32.

In the dark dark I lie listening to Chopin's Préludes, volume low, headphones on to feel vibration: skull, spine, finger, sacrum: to enter again my mother's body: here is the night: twenty-four préludes, everything begun but unfinished: Joelle, my sister, cheeks flushed, lips rosy, the sweet almond scent of her that day at the rest stop: wounded bird, snared coyote: a gun drawn but not fired: the whoopelings of quail in early morning: a lovely looping line crossing and recrossing, no beginning or end, some strange magic: flight of the hawk or snake coiling, a wave of sound inside a stone, breath moving between bodies:

Your wife can't walk: please, for the baby:

A world of sound: the endless rearrangement of notes in space, the infinite possibilities of their relationships to one another: a truck that swerves in time: ocotillo in flame, palo verde in blossom: the heart of a hummingbird beating ten times per second: *Lewis*: there is a hole in the heart of the fetus where blood flows one atrium to the other:

Noemí, Nazario, their baby Idalia: Claire presses your cell phone to her ear, to feel you speak: *sound is touch*:

Lewis:

Nine pints of blood lost, nine poured back into you:

The disappeared speak in trill, in ripple and murmur:

Who would you not save: what being is unworthy?

The disappeared flood your heart:

Their voices are love, birdsong and water:

Lewis:

You hear the whisper of strangers' blood surging through you.

translation

Love is life. All, everything that I understand,
I understand only because I love.
Everything is, everything exists,
only because I love.

—*Leo Tolstoy*

My students speak twenty-nine languages: Javanese, Kikuya, Navajo, Farsi. They come from Kosovo, Cambodia, Belize, Zimbabwe—Laos, Rwanda, Estonia, Uruguay. They have survived malaria and tuberculosis, influenza, dengue fever. They have lived beyond earthquake and famine, fire and flood, drought and tsunami. My children at the literacy center in Salt Lake City have witnessed what they will never understand: their own people murdering one another.

They have stories to tell, but language fails them.

Together we have painted a mural that circles the room: night into day, rainforest to desert, up to the white Himalayas, down to the blue-green ocean. A wide river runs through it all, bringing us here, together. Everywhere you look you find another tiny face: poison arrow frog, coiled cobra, pink flamingo, Chihuahuan raven—black baboons and golden lemurs—scarlet ibis, vervet monkeys—a tortoise swimming in the sand, an owl that looks prehistoric—leopard, lion, fallow deer, fish flying in the tree tops—a luna moth with no mouth, one sweet-smiling camel.

Behind every stone and tree, another almost human child appears as shadow, ready to flee in fear or leap out and kill you.

Last week, two nine-year-old girls and one small boy who survived a fire in their school in Guadalajara came prepared to dance, because they said, *We have no words to tell it.*

They were only children wearing bicycle helmets, little firefighters with flashlights, illuminating our stunned faces one by one—tiny dancers finding sacks of flour, using all their strength to lift the bodies of their friends and carry them outside to weeping parents—three sad survivors crawling down hallways, choking on an illusion of smoke, discovering one slumped teacher who might live if only they could drag her out together.

They wanted us to witness their grief, to feel the weight of loss in their little bodies, the weightlessness of love for the dead who come as smoke and air, who are forever with us. They cradled the sacks or lifted them to their shoulders. They gave us hope in the face of despair: they believed to the end of time they might find one child crouched in the dark, blinded by fear and flame, still miraculously breathing.

They gave me faith: their silent bodies said, *All things by love are possible.* I saw through the veil of smoke: you and you and I—all who have known harm, all who have given grief, all who have touched terror—might dance our story one day so that each could see what the other suffered. We might let our bodies speak the truth, and take turns carrying one another.

requiem: home:
and the rain, after

I had the idea that the world's so full of pain
it must sometimes make a kind of singing.
And that the sequence helps, as much as order helps—
First an ego, and then pain, and then the singing.

—*Robert Hass*
from "Faint Music"

I.

Dangerous to watch the news—
a woman drowned
in a flooded wash,
a girl setting herself on fire—

any blistering day
a mother might forget

the baby in the hot car—
hide her baby
in the trash or trunk—

lose the baby in the stroller in the park.

Saviors with blades
of steel and green
masks might cut a baby

from a deep drain, the hole
in the floor where his mother
flushed him.

She comes to your room at night, red hair a flame, thin
wrists shackled—there, in the box by the bed—she could
be nineteen or ninety, bones as fine as yours, soft voice
whispering through you:

No I wouldn't do this.

Any night when fog swells
from the Sound
through the streets,

when the body of the sky
presses close, when fog
fills your throat,

the dark-skinned officer might
appear as breath, as words:
Have you seen:

Can you identify: a man
in a raccoon mask, robbing
a convenience store.

The video stops and starts and plays again. Doesn't show the girl's face, the girl too stunned to move, the speed of a bullet leaving the gun, the girl dropping behind the counter.

Please, the policeman says, as if
he loves you. Dark hands flutter,
open and close, exposing

pale skin of the palm, soft
pink skin of the fingers, everything
strange, hands too big, fingers flexing.

What to do? Where to put them?

Here, on me. Cover my mouth with your hands. Light glints off his smooth, dark scalp. Does he know? Did he go there? *Cover my eyes.* Wounded and dangerous: *nothing but blood to lose*: the suspect shot twice by a state trooper who just happened to stop, who just wanted coffee, some time with the girl, sugar and cream, her mouth, her hands, her eyes, so pretty.

Unlucky man: end of his shift and now the trooper's bleeding too, as is the boy at the back of the store, sprayed by broken glass, a wall of glass shattering behind him: *any information you may have*:

The officer almost says your name :   : opens his tender mouth, exposes pink skin inside, his mouth that way, the teeth, the tongue, nothing but blood to lose: *Please, call us.*

2.

Dangerous to walk down Broadway.

Even now in bright day
a man might pull
his sputtering car

to the curb, *please,* might
choose you, might ask directions.

A white-haired man, a man
with white stubble, a man as old as God

might show you himself,
might offer what he grips
in his hand:

Do you like? Do you want this?

A pigeon falls from a ledge, crumples
to concrete right there in front of you,

tries to stand on thin legs, flutters

and heaves, drops to its side,
dies while you watch it.

Something hard hits your neck—rock or glass, blade
or bullet—shot in the throat, you could be, this

moment—something warm down your throat, something
slick through your fingers—splattered yolk and viscous
white, nothing but this—sharp shell of an egg launched
hard from a window where a boy in a black hood waves and
smiles, where a boy in a raccoon mask grins and vanishes.

All these humans
so close—close
enough to smell,
close enough to touch
you—and no one
sees—sharp shell
of yourself so brittle—
shot in the throat,
you could have been,

but only you and the boy
who disappears know this.

Twenty-seven years gone, and even now your brother might
appear, might shoot and kill—*please, if you know, call us.*

Wild in the blue day, gulls

whirl high, twenty points

of white light, a constellation

of birds, making

and unmaking itself

Here on earth, two sisters slog through the parking lot, hiding in waves of flesh, shackled and thick in human form. Strapped to the back, an oxygen tank weights one down, its long translucent tube a leash, a loop of breath to the other's nose.

3.

Seven times I watched the news, refusing to believe—the man in the raccoon mask, Gabriel, my brother, the gun in the hand, the girl not moving—denied and denied—as a woman in Pripyat might watch images of black rain, blue smoke, orange fire, and insist it can't be true, and never once look out the window.

Twenty-seven years, and in the utter
absence of human life, in the stunned
silence of human voices,
red deer and fierce boar
flourish—in the Exclusion Zone,
in Chernobyl's Zone of Alienation,
the wolf, the lynx, the bear find refuge.

Foxes, polecats, wild horses.
The beaver returns, restores
the marshes. Bison roam the woods.
Bees make glowing honey.

Over the scorched throat
of the reactor, above
but not so far beyond
the sarcophagus
hiding the hot heart
of Chernobyl, home
into the primeval oaks
of the Forbidden Zone,

black storks glide, white bellies
exposed, red beaks flashing.

No human eye to see: a cloud
of birds, a shadow crossing

the earth—and then: light
through leaves—

scattered light everywhere.

Four hundred thousand humans gone—everything gone—cats, dogs, air to breathe, hungry cattle—our father's wheat, our mother's chickens—gone, the horse we loved—fields of grass, early morning—he carried us on his swayed back. The day the day didn't come, we heard the blast of our father's rifle, felt bone pierce brain as our father shot him.

Home, too dangerous to go there—
twenty-seven years, the earth still hot
with radiation. Dolls lie
in the dust, faces pocked, arms
twisted—a world of glass,
windowpanes in shards, china
shattered—birds roost
in your broken home,
thrive in the peace of your open
spaces—birds line their nests

with lace and grass, human hair,
faces, family—
photographs torn by rain,
words of love, letters tattered.

4.

In the park, cherry, hawthorn,
dogwood blossom. Red bark

of the madrone splits
and peels, exposes
smooth green skin, wet flesh
beneath it. Thousands

of miles, continents
and decades removed
from the fires of Chernobyl,

a flock of pigeons flap
and rise, wings so close
they almost touch head
and hip, hand
and shoulder, nothing

but wind and sound, breath
of bird as they surge through me.

No sarcophagus here, no radiation, Gabriel twenty-seven years gone, and still dangerous to go home, to the house where our parents live—not that far—Seattle to Medina, forty-five minutes from my exclusion zone on Capitol Hill to their zone of alienation where everything remains, where everything happens.

Dangerous to cross the water. The floating bridge might tear apart, drift away in three directions, the lake on one side blue and still, waves on the other green and roiling.

> Mother kneels in the garden, digging
> the damp earth, loving the dark soil—
> beetles and wasps—bugs
> with their beautiful names: ambush,
> assassin, big-eyed, pirate—loving
> whoever comes: rove, robber,
> ladybird, soldier—loving earthworms
> most of all, their silent deaf dumb
> way, their perfect pink wet
> blindness—worms opening
> the earth to air and water,
> offering their bodies inside
> and out, eating dirt, leaving
> soil—making everything
> on earth—the fruit,
> the flower—you,
> your brother—strong
> enough to grow,
> to be possible.

I know it can't be true, but even now I believe my sister's bones are here, buried with the bones of the black cat who killed warblers, finches, robins, vireos. The quick little cat with her white face and one white paw killed sparrows and frogs, butterflies, squirrels. She didn't live by our beliefs. The seven-pound feral cat was never ours to name or rule. She killed a thousand mice, a praying mantis, and then one day stunned and tore Gina Leone's birthday bunny.

We could never prove who fed the black cat poison. My brother found her twitching under the porch, biting her tongue, legs rigid, bile black with blood pouring out both ends of her. My brother Gabriel lay in the dirt, in the dark with worms and spiders—stayed with the cat we loved—until she wiped her white face with her white paw—until she was, and then she wasn't.

Yes, our sister here, in the garden: Lily
        who lived thirty weeks

in our mother's womb and nineteen
        days in an incubator, our sister

who never came home, but who might be
        buried with the cat, the frog,

the dove, the squirrel—bones
        as fine as theirs, as bleached, as brittle.

How else can I explain white bleeding hearts along the fence—foxglove, mountain laurel—all these years and now, forever, the curve of my mother's spine, flowering fern, alstroemeria—the spade, the trowel, the earth undone, my mother digging.

Carry a stone in your mouth
until you learn to be silent.

Gabriel filled his mouth
with stones, and then one
by one swallowed.

5.

Home, and my brother might be alive, banished to his room, not grounded, but given time, stones to count and as much time as it takes for contemplation. He's stolen a flashlight from a neighbor's car, a hacksaw from our uncle Eamonn. He's stuffed a box of three-inch nails down his pants at the hardware store. He doesn't want the nails, but he likes the weight of them, the weird bulge—he loves lingering in the store, zipping ahead and spinning around our father who keeps a thousand nails in his shed—ten thousand—nails of every size, nails for every purpose—our father who would gratefully give his son a jab or jig saw, a flashlight with a brilliant beam, his own new steel hammer.

Our father can build a box to bury a cat, a door, a cradle—anything you want, *tell me*, anything your heart desires. With his brother Eamonn, our father frames a whole house—stairs, struts, beams, skylights. They work in bliss, each sensing the other—buzz of saw, syncopation of hammer—any day our father would happily teach his son to use T-square and bevel, would joyfully with him build a house in the trees where a boy might find refuge.

But Gabe wants none of what our father offers. He likes to stuff and stash, to slip inside, to rearrange and redistribute—to take and trash or use and bury—my brother loves dusk and dark and early morning. While we lie paralyzed by sleep, Gabriel flies free, a boy on a silver bike, slashing the dark, the bike a blade, the body blazing.

Home, we have dreamed ourselves to death
and awakened. How else can I explain

bloodroot and violet, my father's
fluttery hands, a confusion of clouds,

lavender, nasturtium,
bees in bliss, broken

light, wisteria climbing
the trellis, scattered light

through leaves, my father's body,
the way his limp and drag

leaves me weak on one side, strange
to myself, wounded, dizzy.

I've seen the scan of the brain, cortex shrunken away from bone, an irradiated vision of my father's mind, lobes shadowed with dark clouds, places where vessels have burst and bled—bullets tearing through the brain, glass shattering inside him—dark spaces where synapses don't spark, where neural networks jolt and sputter.

My dazed father falls down dead and wakes slumped in the shower, water so cold—but why? He can't understand it. My father trips down the stairs, tilts off the ladder. Mother never knows where. The basement? The bedroom?

My befuddled father nails himself in the shed. He loves turpentine and glue, buzz of the saw, wood chips flying. Loves the shock of metal on wood, power drill, angle grinder.

Three 2 x 4's brace the door, twenty-seven nails hold them: my father unsafe inside, losing his mind, losing a finger—something beautiful he wanted to build—bevel, twine, vice grips, pliers—if only how and what—if only he remembered.

6.

Dangerous to have a body, to hurt,
to know the hurt of others. Any day
a father like your own, a man
too much moved by the grief
of strangers might see
another man seize and fall
in a New York subway, might imagine
no choice for himself—blaze
of light, train roaring—might
leap to save and feel hot
wind rushing toward them.

No time to lift, to heave, to struggle—no time to climb from the pit—so he flattens the man instead, pins him between the tracks, presses his body hard on the flailing man, uses his whole human self to hold him down, not knowing if the train will tear through, sever and slice, shred or blast over.

The news tonight: now
we know: centimeters
to spare, howling wind
inside and out, sparks
and cries, everything
so hot, the blistering
back, and then
the dark—and

then, voices.

All that time, all those moments, and here she is, the savior's
seven-year-old daughter alone at the edge of the platform,
heat of her father's hand leaving her hand forever.

Later, in the park,

everything too green—

spikes of grass, blades

of willow—

the birds, the birds,

the birds so noisy.

Her father tries to take her hand, but *no,* she saw him die,
no—she will not let him.

7.

Dangerous to sleep in my parents' house. The night becomes years, the air an ocean. I rock in a narrow bed on the second floor, a child again, in this house forever. Any night I might wake and find my father here, sitting on the edge of my bed, oblivious to me, contemplating the thing he can't name, too beautiful to be, the rhododendron grown so tall he could reach out this window, now, touch its red blossoms. He wants a mind like this, leaves sensing light, roots finding water, the will to be this tall, the faith to grow flowers.

In the Zone of Alienation, saplings
sprout from the kitchen floor,
willows grow through broken windows—

vines climb up the walls
to tear them down later.

Wild grape, feral roses—rain
rots wood to pluck
strings of your piano.

The curved back of the cello
splits and peels, splinters
down the long spine,
sings to itself in the rain, cracks

in the sun, after.

The owl returns from a night's work,
disgorges bones bound
with hair and feathers—

the bear has found your bed unmade,
your doors and roof forever open.

Home, and my brother Gabriel is dead, and it might have been yesterday or not yet, and Gabriel might be alive—camellia, snowdrop, zephyr lily—our sister safe in the womb: now, she could be. Gabriel and I press small hands to Mother's skin, feel tiny elbows jab us.

The cat, the birds, the rabbit, the squirrels—the girl in the convenience store might be alive tonight—if only I hadn't seen—a man in a raccoon mask—the gun, the bullet—if only I hadn't watched the news three times that night and twice the next morning—*please, do you know—call if you see him*—my brother, the girl—and her parents watching too—later, they must have—ten times, a hundred—the video replayed, backward and forward—their little girl rising up, their little girl dropping, and again and before, and my brother in the mask, and the girl almost smiling.

Home, the forbidden zone, where everything
can be or not be—where rain on the roof,
where maple, where magnolia—
where everything blooms—iris,
lobelia—where everything you love
grows dangerously feral.

8.

To ourselves and others, we were known not as Pelia, Vassia, Viktor, Volodya—not Tolik, Eduard, Igor, Gregori—not as seven hundred thousand separate souls, but as one, as liquidators.

In the beginning, we were on the roof of Reactor Three, heaving shovels full of debris into the heart of the fire. Ninety seconds was a lifetime's work, a thousand years of radiation.

For the sacrifice of our bodies, we received medals with drops of blood and the signs we now know as our own, particles and rays—Alpha, Beta, Gamma—we were radioactive waste, heroes of the state, dangerous to wives and doctors, children in the womb, children not imagined. We offered our bodies inside and out. Some of us died fast, and some refused to die and didn't. Our bodies were secrets of the state—skin burned black, flesh crackling—our lungs came out our mouths—our hearts, our livers—our bowels dissolved—our tongues split in our mouths—our mouths peeled off in layers.

If we were among the lucky, blessed enough to die, they buried us in wood and zinc, lead and plastic. Twenty-seven years and even now our bodies glow underground. Even now our hair could kill you.

Dangerous, the dead—
our radioactive bodies speak
their own language.

Again I watched the news, still denying the man in a raccoon mask, Gabriel, my brother—refusing the body—as a woman in Pripyat might see a ravaged face and say, *No, that's not my husband.*

But I know my brother's hands,
line of the jaw, narrow shoulders—
my brother's fractured skull,
my brother's broken
pelvis—where Gabriel hurts
and hurts, where bones fuse
but never heal.

The dark-skinned officer comes again
and again, there in the box
by the bed—his tongue, his teeth,
his hands, his fingers, *please*—
we can't sleep, pink skin
of the mouth, the mouth open.

Not Vladimir, Alyosha, Sergei, Gennady—not Valentin, Ivan, Nicolai, Dimitri—we were one, we came after—after rain, after fire—after the humans were gone, four hundred thousand gone—removed, evacuated, gone—forbidden to return because here, on this earth, the soil is dangerous—the hair of your cat, the bones of your terrier—mushrooms bloom in the brain—the geraniums, the berries—the dust on the leaves destroys the throat as you breathe it.

Everything will kill, everything poison.
Everything you love we came to bury.

No, not true, not Gabriel. A night and a day and the morning and the news and the officer still asking. Seven times he came to my room before I confessed—*yes, I do: yes, I know him*—my heart crazy in my chest, my brother's blood roaring. I thought I would die driving to my parents' house, heart hammering itself dumb, the floating bridge sinking, and then home and there she was, Mother kneeling in the garden.

We buried the earth, cut into the soil and rolled the earth like a rug—grass, flowers, worms, beetles—heaved the earth into shallow graves, buried the earth with ants and spiders. We sawed trees and buried forests—eggs, milk, wells, gardens. You left a note on the door:

Please don't hurt the cat.
She kills the voles. She helps
the garden. Dear, kind Person,
Use whatever you need,
but please, don't trash the house.

We'll be home soon.
We'll come home later.

We dug a pit on the side of your house. We buried your house in the pit. We buried your village.

You can't come home to the Zone. The Zone is off limits. We photographed ourselves in your vacant houses. We ate the canned beans. We ate the canned cherries.

> *Dear, kind Person,*
> *Use whatever you need.*

We shot your cats and dogs. Their fur, their breath, their tongues—dangerous.

Why speak now? The human mind is not enough to understand it.

Before we came, your dogs and cats ate eggs, then chickens—cucumbers, tomatoes—then the dogs ate the cats, and the cats ate their babies. We came to save. We came to deliver. The horse knew everything. The white horse cried when we took him to the field.

Some of us liked to kill, and some were sick after. We drank vodka to kill, and vodka to protect us from radiation. In the beginning your dogs ran toward us, but later they growled and charged. They showed us their terrible teeth, and we had to kill your dogs because everything you love grows feral.

9.

All these years, and Mother always here, loving worms, loving spiders, anyone who comes—rove, robber, me, my brother—the feral cat, the frogs, the finches—all these years, backward and forward, cypress and holly, and my father at the door, so straight and strong that day, so beautiful, and the light on his face, *my God*, my father so glad to see me.

Home, and my brother might be in the shed, eating fire, extinguishing matches till his mouth is scorched. He loves anything that hurts—leaping from the roof, flying from the maple—slamming hard into the ground, spinning all day after.

We slaughtered your chickens in the barn, so much noise, so many feathers. We tried to close our eyes. We saw through closed eyelids.

I sat at my parents' kitchen table. I drank their coffee. I dunked my toast. I tried to swallow. *So blue,* I said, *and gulls whirling—the drive across the bridge today, the light and everything so beautiful—and look, your rhododendron, so red, so many blossoms*—and Mother said, *why*—and I said, *I think Gabe's in trouble*, and, *have you seen the news*, and then light shattered through the glass, and I heard every window breaking—felt the house crushed, saw the garden buried—the maple tree cut down—the rhododendron hacked and killed, plowed into the earth—the camellia, the cherry. *Please*, my mother said, meaning don't say, don't tell us—meaning that without words none of this could be, none of this would happen.

No: as if Gabe never lost twenty pounds in juvenile detention. Twenty pounds in forty days—because the other boys were bigger than Gabe and so hungry—because you can make a knife with a scrap of wood, paper and spit, broken plastic—because you can scoop out a boy's eye with a spoon, *so why not just give us your dinner?*

Please—as if Gabe never fractured his own skull in prison—Gabriel down for five in Walla Walla, a nineteen-year-old man, an adult now, convicted of breaking and entering, eating and drinking, living house to boat and boat to trailer, wherever he could find a bed, a bath, a bottle, leather boots, Darvon and oxycodone—wherever he could score Nembutal and bronchodilators.

Five years and kept here, alone, apart, in isolation, six hundred and twenty-two days of his eighteen hundred and fifty-seven.

Alone—for his own good, for his own protection:

because you provoked
because impulses

because the bodies of other men

because you flooded the tier
flushing and flushing

because someone there
look, a face in the water

because you opened a vein with a staple

because you didn't stop
because you couldn't

and the skin inside your throat
look, blood and spit in the water

and the skin pulled inside out
as other bodies broke through you

Please. As if my brother locked alone in his cell didn't refuse food, didn't talk to the face in the toilet, didn't squat instead in the corner—as if Gabriel didn't find a way to stop all fear, to end all voices, to never hurt, to never want anything—as if the boy we loved didn't bash the head to the floor, pain to end all pain, until the skull split open, as if the brain didn't fester and burn, hot with infection.

Gabriel loves vodka and Valium, angel dust and crushed amphetamines, crack and coke chased by heroin—the heat, the hurt—anything to slow the heart, anything to charge and jolt it. He loves the vein, the hit, the blood, the needle, the hours gone, the days buried.

In the cell, in the dark, in the dirt,
after, Gabriel befriended a spider
with beautiful long legs and
a round fat belly—seven legs

because somewhere in her life
she'd lost one. He loved her
pale skin. He saw inside
and through her. Nothing
was not her. Tiny
as she was, she filled the room.
She ate him. Brain
so hot, bowels burning—*please*:
the throat too scorched
to drink and so thirsty.

He let her lay her eggs in his bed, let her children feast on his body—

because blood not mine to hold, cracked
skin not keeping myself inside it.

Please, as if *no,* as if *never,* as if our mother doesn't believe Gabriel lives in the jungle under the freeway with pigeons and gulls, feral cats and coyotes—as if she herself hasn't seen Gabriel, her son, pulling fish heads from trash, bruised fruit at Pike's Market. *No,* as if any day, Gabriel might come home, might arrive, any moment.

The apple tree bloomed. The lilac flowered—rose, jasmine, poppy, lily—everything alive, but strange—the day blue and still, but we couldn't smell the blossoms. We worked twelve-hour shifts. We gave our blood. We drank your vodka. We killed everything that moved, and then everything that didn't. And then one day we were standing in the forest, and we saw a hundred ants on a single branch, ten thousand on one slender birch tree. We saw spiders and worms, all going their way, each with some purpose. We didn't know their names. We didn't know their children. We were seven hundred thousand beings, so many human beings, and still our human lives meant nothing. We began to understand the infinities of lives lost, the ones we killed, the ones we buried. If you learn to love this way, the whole world destroys you.

10.

I turned on the news at noon. I meant to prove it. And there he was, undeniable: a feral dog slipping through the automatic doors of the grocery store, flashing down the aisle for pampered pets where he snatched a rawhide bone, where a manager in red blocked his path—as if to reason or detain, make him drop the bone, march him safely out of here.

> But no: he's quick, he's gone.
> Black streak, blurred shadow:
> the dog bounding
>
> out the double doors, down
> alleys, through culverts,
>
> a wolf in the woods,
> free in the world, happily
>
> gnawing his bone in a jungle
> of roots and vines, with cats
> and crows under the freeway.

This was the news at noon, the failure to find a feral animal.

But my father said, *We need to tell the police. I need to see the video.* Because he knew what I said was true—because through Gabriel, his son, everything on earth had become possible.

My mother opened the window wide. My mother wouldn't go with us.

We saw an old woman walking into the woods with her starved cow and twelve chickens. They were all she had—her home, her family—we let them go. If we didn't speak the truth, nothing here could harm them.

II.

Twenty-seven years and still dangerous to go to work.
The body of the brain-injured boy is a living text, thorns
and doves, red slashes—the beatitudes inscribed, a prayer
pierced into him. I'm teaching the twenty-four-year-old
boy to sing because he can't speak, because he collided with
a tree, flying on his snowboard. I'm helping him hear the
intonation of vowels, how long to hold them—buzz of saw,
syncopation of hammer—we're tapping out a rhythm with
our left hands, finding the flow of thought, pitch and timbre,
words as waves, the river of language.

The boy opens his tattooed arms, and in his perfect silence
asks me to sing the scars:

Blessed are the pierced by love
Blessed the slashed with mercy

Here is my brother's body, lying in a bed of ferns and trash
under the freeway—my brother, a heap of rags, wet grass,
bloody feathers—Gabriel bleeding out but not yet gone,
the jaw shot away on one side and something under the ribs
leaking—the first bullet into the face, but the second only
grazed him.

No words now, rush of cars, blood roaring.

Blessed the ones struck
by strokes—shrapnel, trees,
shattering windshields—

the ones I teach to sing
after blades, after bullets—
after the brain bleeds

into itself—lesions, tumors,
hemangiomas—after the skull

fractures—
blessed the ones who want to sing,

after rain, after sorrow, after
vessels in the brain explode,
and the world comes apart inside them.

My father and I watched the video thirteen times, stopping
and starting, backward and forward, and again and before,
and the girl not afraid of the man in the raccoon mask
and black hood, just a kid off the street, a joke, and the
girl almost smiling—her mouth that way, so pretty and
the gun pulled from the pocket, and my brother's hand
trembling—and there's a boy at the back of the store,
snatching Twinkies, a boy slipping a can of Coke inside his
jacket, sliding a plastic pistol down his pants, stuffing a tiny
soldier in his pocket—and my brother is asking for the cash
and the girl looks confused—

words don't work

—and maybe there's an alarm—

and words are spit and senses sputter

—and the gun is going off and the girl is dropping and the girl is rising up—and the throat and the bullet—and again and she's gone and there must be a sound, a cry, a voice from the back of the store loud enough to make my brother spin and fire—and the glass behind the boy explodes and the glass rises up in shards and all its broken pieces heal—

and again

—and the boy drops the Coke and the wall of glass splinters and the glass is shooting into the boy and the boy like the girl is dropping—

Blessed the ones who grieve
who hunger now for refuge

I wanted the dark-skinned officer to appear, to come into this room, to say our names out loud, to love and then forgive us. If he refused his mercy now, I wanted the fog of that other night to hide and then to fill us.

12.

Where to look, how to find him? The detective asks again, as if we've known all along, as if now in this room he and the light above might force our confession.

Gabriel lived in a cardboard box under the freeway, but one night he was smoking in the box and the box caught fire. He built a house of sticks and covered it with four slit trash bags, but the wind took one bag and then another, rain poured through the roof, the roof collapsed, the house rotted. So he made a nest of ferns and lined it with rags and feathers. Look for him here where rats grow big as rabbits.

If he contacts you...

My father could tell him nineteen months since they'd heard from Gabriel—if the detective called my mother, she could count the days, give an exact number—could describe the morning he left, light on the table, trembling hands, tea spilled in the saucer, scrambled eggs he couldn't eat—she could tell him, *I scraped the eggs into the trash, and Gabriel said, I'm sorry.*

My father could whisper, *Sometimes I leave the car unlocked, two twenties in the glove box. Sometimes his mother opens a window in the kitchen, leaves a cherry pie with a note on the table. We walk in our sleep. We eat. We steal. We lie to ourselves. We lie with each other.*

And then we were driving home, the day still blue, gulls whirling, impossible to believe—I cracked the window, and yes, it was true, the wind out there still blowing, and the bridge did come apart; I felt the bridge beneath us sinking. But I refused to stop. I kept driving. A long blue car passed in the left lane, two little girls kneeling in the back unbelted—blonde, bobbing girls waving and smiling.

They kissed their small hands and blew kisses out to us. I thought we would die. I tasted blood in my throat, felt vessels exploding.

My heart had stopped. I thought, *I'm not breathing.* My father covered his face with both hands. The little girls bounced in delight, a game—they had fallen in love with him.

Their mother turned to scold, to get them back in their belts, to save us.

I took my father home. We sat in the driveway. Impossible to go inside, but then we did, and I stood in the living room while he went upstairs to find my mother. They didn't come down. I couldn't hear them. I sat at the piano and there we were in the big green chair, two-year-old Gabe holding one-year-old Nora, our mouths the same, so pink, both open, and our ears so small, our ears so perfect, and our parents upstairs, *now,* so quiet.

What I wanted was to climb the stairs, to lie on the bed between, to feel time spin backward, to know myself small, to be myself nothing, to sense my brother and sister and self as undreamed dreams inside our parents' bodies.

I put the photograph in my purse so it wouldn't kill them. Then I was driving home and the bridge was whole, the bridge had healed, and I thought, *I can make it home,* but I didn't. I stopped in a church, not to pray, but to use the bathroom because ridiculous as it seems the body has needs, the body has hunger—the body is full of blood and piss—the body has urges and obligations.

There, in the basement of the church, I thought, *No one knows. No one needs to know, ever.* I sat in the dark stall. I made my confession. I asked God to save my brother's life. I asked God, *Please, take him.* I heard voices on the stairs, ripples of laughter—girls on the stairs—so loud, so oblivious. They didn't notice the closed door of the stall, could never imagine me, a woman who has watched her brother shoot a girl in the throat, a girl like them, thirteen times in the throat—has watched with her father—backward and forward—he can shoot all day and all night—he'll do this forever. They were laughing and changing their clothes. They'd found a bag of clothes in a trash bin. *How can you? Someone else's filthy clothes. Blood and piss. You don't know what. Some stranger's skin on your body.*

Two girls left one behind, there at the sink when I came out, a girl trying to be and not be pretty, each ear pierced five times, soft lobe to thick cartilage, fishnets torn, black boots for stomping, a girl painting blue-black lines around her eyes, smudging them to dark bruises. The streaked face in the mirror behind her face startled both of us. So old I was, bare face so naked. The orange dress she'd found fit too tight for her to zip alone. *Do you mind, will you please, can you help me?* Her voice that way, low and soft, swirling inside, touching my eardrum.

She wanted me to put my hands on her.
She wasn't afraid. She didn't know anything.
I did what she asked. Cold hands trembling.
And her skin was soft, *my God,* soft as God's
if God had a body, soft as my sister's
in the womb, and even God
held his breath while she sucked her belly
firm and I zipped her, and my sister
lay in the earth, not that deep
in the garden, stones in her mouth,
stones in her belly, yellow tulips
waving in the wind above, stones
nested in her ribcage, stones smooth
as eggs cradled in her tiny pelvis, *Lily,*
blue sky and tulips full of light,
and down below worms and spiders.

13.

Twenty-seven years and still dangerous to drift through
the grocery store where a girl in a glittery tutu and tattered
sweater needs the full force of her fifty pounds to push a
shriveled woman in a wheelchair down long aisles. The
brother swoops up and down, dancing behind, spinning
around them—a Nijinsky at twelve, swirling a box of
popcorn under his black cape—cheese to squirt from a can,
chocolate chips, chocolate cookies—

> Who will want to see?
> Who will dare to stop them?

Grandma buys hot dogs, Fruit Loops, sparkling grape
juice—a liter of Mountain Dew, chicken pies, frozen waffles.
She buys two dozen eggs, enough beautiful white-shelled
eggs for the boy to slip three up his sleeve to launch at me
from his window.

> With his black cape and raccoon mask,
> the boy we love believes he's invisible.

14.

Dangerous to imagine:
a house dark on Beacon Hill,
a basement window cracked open—

my brother finding refuge
from the rain, sweet
surprise, a girl's bedroom—

window raised to let smoke
drift out, but resin soaked
every particle.

He dumped drawers, ripped clothes from hangers, plunged hands through every fold, fingers down every pocket, collected two dollars and twenty-nine cents, but recovered no hash or pipe, no buds, no papers.

Dangerous to be a bear on the bed,
to see, to witness: the girl
flung to the floor—clothes trashed
and torn, dirty hands everywhere.

Gabriel slit the belly of the bear, spilled a jumble of tattered bowel while stitched eyes stared into him.

Upstairs he found four packs of cigarettes, three Diet Cokes, a five and a ten tucked in a jar, whipped cream in a can, a bag of Oreos.

Anything you want, tell me,
anything your heart desires.

He grabbed a frosted bottle of Stolichnaya from the freezer, so cold it burned the hand, so cold down the throat his heart stuttered.

In a bathroom on the second floor, the medicine cabinet provided blue pills for menstrual pain and pink ones for motion sickness. He thought both might help, especially with the vodka. He took the box of Benadryl, cough syrup with codeine, mouthwash and toothpaste, a towel to hold it all, the woman's comb and yellow toothbrush.

Dangerous to know, to sense,
to see my brother in the bedroom,
falling in love with the scent
of a woman, smoke and lavender
in the clothes, in the closet—
no need to go out in the rain—
in the drawers, on the pillowcase—
when he can swallow the pills
now, drink the syrup down, stop
and rest, sleep or die here.

He took the woman's pillowcase—to carry his stash, to clutch in the dark, to hold in a bed of ferns, in the rain, after.

Dangerous to find a little gun
wrapped in a red rag, tucked
in the drawer of the nightstand—

anything you want, tell me—

a compact Beretta, *your heart's*
unknown desire, loaded,
for you, because a woman
and a girl alone need
something to protect them—

And look, to be safe, to be sure: two boxes of ammunition.

Good God, how many intruders did she want to come here? If she'd been in the bed tonight, she would have killed him.

Crazy as it was, he stopped to brush his teeth, here, at a clean sink with running water—spit and blood, gums so sore he almost wept, teeth so tender. He scorched his mouth with Listerine. He burned his throat. He swallowed. In the kitchen, he took a handful of the woman's pills and chased them down with vodka.

The cold was cold and the rain
pelted, but he was safe
for the night, already high,
almost delivered.

Home, under the freeway, he traded the Stolichnaya and two packs of cigarettes for five Demerol, and he was good, and his blood was rain, his bones water.

Gabriel, my brother—
one day we ran out in the rain
just as the rain started—
we lay down in the street,
let the rain be the rain,
warm drops then cold pellets—
we stood shivering
in the rain
to see our bodies
bare on the street,
the dry places
we'd been, to know
our borders—we watched
our selves pocked
and filled with rain,
our selves gone,
our bodies
vanishing.

Inside we stripped
our clothes—so cold
we couldn't speak,
so cold
we took a bath together.

15.

Two nights of peace and a day hollowed out and hungry. The last dollars spent on three hits of speed that must have been laced with rat poison and baby laxative. Empty now, evacuated, and the night had come again, like God, always, and my brother out in the rain, and the gun, small and light as it was, tilting him off balance.

Everything hurt: burned hand, bowels, belly—the teeth most of all, and *my God*, after the bad speed so hungry. If he used the gun in a convenience store, he could have anything he wanted, cash from the drawer and as many cigarettes as he could carry.

But he wasn't ready for that, hoped he wouldn't be, ever—he was scared of the gun, remembering a golden squirrel chattering from a tree in the ravine, hair full of light, a slingshot, a stone, his ridiculous luck, the squirrel falling, lying in leaves, quiet but not dead, black eyes watching—nothing to do but crush the skull, and no wonder now his own skull throbbing, and the belly of the bear slit, so yes, no wonder, hungry too, and the girl finding the bear under her bed, stitching the wound closed, promising to kill whoever had done this.

Hunched against the rain, Gabriel cruised through parking lots looking for an unlocked door, a car where he might catch a minute's rest, where the rain couldn't touch, where he might be warmer. Three lots and half a mile in the rain before he found a black truck outside a bar, nine cigarettes left in a pack in the glove box.

He wanted to smoke in the truck, one cigarette after another, fill the cab with fumes till he was sick with smoke and could float out of here. One cigarette, five minutes—he decided to take the risk, and *God,* it was good, the sweetest thing he could remember. He started to light the second from the first, but the man was there, opening the door, grabbing his arm, yanking him from the truck, kicking him to the pavement, and the gun was out, in Gabe's hand, and the man was backing away, *no problem,* and Gabe heard himself say, *oh, there is a problem,* and he saw himself from above, as if watching a movie: a wet, ragged scrap of a man holding a gun on another human being in a parking lot, lights from poles diffused by rain, everything fuzzy, a performance of himself, who he is, what he's becoming, and he knows he should stop or laugh, but *God,* his stomach hurts, and he can't eat, not now, maybe never, the teeth throbbing to the roots, gums so sore, gums bleeding, and the stomach inside out, the stomach shriveled, and the pills from the woman's house made everything worse, and the speed almost killed him, and the cigarettes left in the pack, *God,* seven cigarettes might save him.

In a voice that must be his he hears someone telling the man to get down, *on your knees,* and the rain pelts them both and the man kneels and he's telling the man, *very slow now, your wallet,* and he can't believe this is him, because he sounds so preposterous, but yes, it's true, he's here, this is happening, and even now he knows he should get down on his own knees, ask the man for forgiveness, give the gun to the man, let him decide what to do here, but *no,* the voice inside, very soft, *this is easy,* and the man outweighs him by fifty pounds—without the gun, the man would kill him, and he remembers three boys in juvenile detention, the ones who ate his dinner day after day, forty days, *because you can scoop out an eye with a spoon,* and even now he's so hungry, and his head hurts, and his bowels twisting, and the boys' bodies close, and the boys' bodies pressed against him, and he backs away with the wallet and cigarettes, pulls the cash out, turns and sprints, drops the wallet, can't believe he can run, so scared, so happy.

16.

Blessed are you who hunger. Impossible as he seems, I did not invent the boy with the beatitudes inscribed on his body. *Blessed the slashed by mercy.* Twenty-seven years I've been waiting for one like him to come bearing this message, but never did I imagine the body pierced, a child lying still so many hours, each jab of the needle a way to know God beyond all language, to have the words, but not need them. Ten thousand, a hundred thousand—how many times was he stabbed? Only God knows. Only God kept counting.

Ninety-two dollars in the man's wallet, enough to score in Freeway Park, *concrete heaven,* safe and saved, tangle of roads so close, rush of cars drowned by water. Gabriel loves this place, the way sound opens and kills, comes inside to kill and calm him.

His works long gone so he has to snort the dope, a snowball of coke and heroin, and it's good, and he loves the bitter drip down the back of the throat, the best taste he can imagine, and the dope might be cut with strychnine, and the coke might be mostly Novocaine, but he's high now and he's on his way home, to his nest of leaves and rags, to rats and crows, feral dogs, his friends, pigeons and gulls, and *now* is all there is, and the dope will get him through a day and another night, and *after* is beyond, not now, maybe never.

Blessed are you who grieve. Twenty-seven years later I'm humming to the brain-injured boy. On a notepad I write: *No words today, just music.* I hum a question that might be:

Are you hungry? or: *Do you love me?* He raises one hand and makes a sound like a bird, deep in the throat, two sounds at once, a whoop and a warble. I take this to mean he wants to go outside, and I hum the question, and *yes*, he does, and we go out in the world where leaves are green flames and birds yellow fire.

17.

Four hundred thousand humans gone, evacuated from the Zone, forbidden to return to their radioactive farms, their dangerous gardens. In the villages we didn't bury, the weight of snow collapsed roofs, fire tore through splintered rafters. We thought nothing could survive. The bones of animals would bear no weight; the eggs of birds would crack and crumble. Sterile or mutant, everything strange, but no one told the storks, and no one told the weasels. They loved this new world, the earth wet without humans.

Beavers appeared by the hundreds and thousands. They worked day after day, damming man-made canals, tunneling under dikes, restoring marshes for frogs and moose, egrets and cormorants—mosquitoes, gnats, otters, turtles—returning farms to wilderness faster than any human dared imagine—decades of work undone—and soon the fox returned to hunt vole and rabbit. Bear and badger came—eagle, falcon. The boar grew fat, too fat to kill, and wolves returned but feared to stalk him.

Snow melted in the Carpathian Mountains and flowed four hundred miles northeast to flood abandoned fields. Without canals or dikes to slow the water, the Pripyat River rose twenty-five feet and spread ten miles. And the beaver saw that it was good, and with his holy work continued.

In the Exclusion Zone, time spins backward.

18.

Down in the jungle under the freeway, deep in his zone of alienation, high and happy and not hurt while the dope lasted, at peace with feral cats who have learned perfect silence, Gabriel lost track of time and knew day and night, the sound of rain, clouds passing, and everything was good, rats no less than dogs, dogs no less than humans till he woke into a day of terrible light, the dope gone, the bag empty, nothing left to lick, the tongue sore, he'd done that—till everything returned as it was—fractured skull, broken pelvis—as if shattered just now, as if again cracked and splintered—because the body knows, the bones remember, the body returns you to yourself and turns the eye inward. The body feeds on the starved heart. Food will not enter the shriveled stomach. Tiny hands clench the bowel, wring and twist tighter and tighter.

And the fog comes, and the night hides you,
and you go out in a cloud of fog to find
the one thing that will save you.

19.

Home, and I might be unsafe
in our mother's womb,
and the sound of the rain tonight
is a song strung
through my brother's body,
Gabriel ten months old, wild
in the rain, howling
in his crib, terrified of lightning—

the whole sky lit
between clouds, explosions
brighter than day,
and then explosions
of thunder, everything
on earth struck, all
light and sound, everything
vibrating, strut
and beam, spine and
ribcage, everything rain,
flooding our bodies.

Gabriel pulls himself up in the crib and Mother finds him clenching the bars of his cage—his tiny body, the crib, everything rattling—my brother's impossible strength: all nerve and bone, muscle electrified.

He will not be consoled. Will not be comforted. Mother heavy with me and so tired, but she carries us up and down the hall, one twisting in the womb, and my brother in her arms wailing.

> Nothing now will calm.
> No one now can soothe us.

I swear it's true though I'm told it's not possible: I remember the lightning that night, not bolts or forks, but blasts of light, the world irradiated. Through flesh and blood and water, I saw the light, knew my brother as myself, felt our bones shimmer.

The gun in the hand in the pocket—this too I know, this too I feel—and the girl doesn't believe and says *no* or only hesitates and we pull the gun out—not to shoot but to show her. I can see in the video how she shakes her head, disbelieving: *This is me—this is now—I'm going to die for two hundred dollars*. And we hear the pop of the gun, and she drops just like that, not a girl, but a body, and the boy yelps and we spin, and the gun hot in the hand, spraying bullets, and the trooper opens the door wide, thinking of the girl, *yes*: he steps into the light, not knowing.

> We have one shot left for him, and he has two for us
> as our body by some miracle of light or luck
> leaps through the open door and the fog takes us.

20.

I play the video backward, and look, here's the trooper, not walking into the store, but backing out of it, sliding into the cruiser, long legs and black boots, Micah Dean, just off duty, thirty-six years old and yes, married, but he can't go home, not yet, can't bear to be there, *no*: the empty bed, the smell of his wife's hair still on the pillow, the door to his little girl's room closed, and no one listening in the dark, no small voice to whisper, *Daddy*.

Home—where he sleeps on the couch even now because the smell and her imprint and the words in the walls in the bedroom:

It's not what you think. And he said, *I wouldn't dare imagine.*

See, that's why, and she meant his voice, not the words but the rhythm—the intent, the intonation—she meant black boots by the door, gun in the holster—*and God,* his hands on her—*everything so quick—like being shoved in a cruiser.*

Then she was sorry, in a way, and she said, *Some time, some space, we'll talk later—I promise.*

Fifteen days and no words with her, but Susana calls once a week to say when he can pick her up, how long he can keep her. So yes, who can blame him—he's fallen in love with a pretty girl in a convenience store. Three times he's come, and twice she's been here, and he's smiling in the cruiser, checking himself in the mirror, not really in love—all he wants is some kindness, coffee with cream—extra cream, extra sugar—and her tongue and her teeth—and he's out of the cruiser again, opening the door where so many things have already happened.

He gets off three shots and two find my brother, and the blast through the jaw feels like the whole head exploding, but the hand holds the gun, and the finger pulls the trigger, and the trooper takes a hit in the knee, and the earth now is trembling.

The video spins, backward again, and look, shards of glass are flying not in but out of the boy's body—so beautifully wounds close, so perfectly glass heals—and the boy slides Twinkies back on the shelf, slips a can of Coke into the cooler, pulls a plastic pistol from his pants, tenderly untucks a tiny soldier from his pocket. Even the thought of theft swirls out of him, and look, the boy is backing out of the store, riding his red bike in reverse, climbing backward through the bedroom window.

Kevin Petilla: who can believe a child so good, a body so agile?

No fight with his mother, no fires at school, no little girl saying she saw, no false accusations—no slap, no hit, no leaping out of the car, no concussion, no bruises—no policeman bringing him home in cuffs: *To teach you a lesson.*

Everything dissipates in fog, *gone,* into a vast cloud of unknowing.

And my brother spins back toward the place where the girl stood behind the counter. There are a billion cells in the heart, thirty billion ion channels. Every moment of her beautiful life each one has worked perfectly. And look, she's unfolding, rising up from the floor, and the bullet leaves the throat and returns to the pistol, and my brother slips the gun in the pocket, and the girl, *my God,* this time he sees her—pale skin and teeth so perfect—she's not afraid: she's almost smiling—and he's not going to do this thing—*no,* he's winding backward down the aisles, unwalking a bright labyrinth, stepping backward into fog where the cloud of fog receives him.

Home, and I am safe
in our mother's womb.
The lightning has stopped,
but the rain continues.

And Mother sits with us
in the swing on the porch,
me not kicking and Gabriel
not wailing, and my love
for my brother is
the sound of the rain—
camellia, rhododendron,
wisteria, maple—the way
rain touches leaves—
mock orange
and magnolia.

My brother has found his way home, has plunged through fog, holding the shattered jaw with one hand, as if the hand can contain him. Now he stumbles on tangled roots—now he falls and surrenders. And rats smell his blood, but feral cats come to protect him.

21.

In the Zone of Alienation, bison return to the forest—black storks, wild horses. We did not imagine these beings. The human mind did not invent them.

A billion cells in my brother's heart now by the hundreds of thousands failing. Darkness and day and a dog howling and the body free of its pain—he knows not what he's done—and the fog of the night gone and the light touching his face and the wings of birds by light illuminated.

> *Blessed are the poor in spirit, the ones*
> *who have and want and are nothing.*

Thirty billion ion channels and now not one sparks the heart. Now not even God can save us.

> Dangerous to answer the phone—
> *we found a body*—dumped
> at the side of the road,
> wrapped in a red blanket,
> feet bare, face shattered—
> and yes, we will come, my mother
> and father and I, and yes will know
> beyond all doubt and disbelief
> the feet, the hands, the clavicle, the child.

Where to go now, what to do after? I sleep in a narrow bed in my parents' house. I rock in my cradle. I dream a feral dog,

a black dog with a glorious tail, the first to understand—
unafraid, he sniffs my brother.

And the night has come again, and the dog
howling, a cry sweet and loud enough
to wake the dead, but even the dog
with his miraculous voice can't do it.

Three humans come to find out why, to make him quiet, to
discover not to their surprise another human mind gone,
another human body broken.

Be not afraid:
Last week a man tossed
like a bag of trash, flung
thirty feet, overpass to jungle.

And the week before that
a woman beaten by boys,
and not yet dead, set on fire.

If they've not killed
or been killed,
they've just been lucky.

Blessed are the ones who surrender,
who ask not why, who do what is needed.

These three, two men and a woman, make a sling with a blanket to carry the dead man from the jungle to the highway because battered as the body is, someone in the world might know, someone out there might still love him.

The slope is steep and the body, wasted as it is, surprisingly heavy. They set him down five times, and any one of the three might say, *enough*, but no one speaks, and with the black dog bounding ahead and back and in circles around them, they carry the dead man to the road and leave him there, swaddled in a dirty blanket.

22.

Thirty-six days later, when the news of Chernobyl reached us, when whirling winds carried radioactive particles to Poland, Germany, Austria, Romania—Switzerland, France, Belgium, India—England, Greece, Israel, Canada—Kuwait, Japan, Turkey, America—when radioactive rain fell on Waterford, Ireland—when thousands of poisoned reindeer in Scandinavia were oh-so-mercifully slaughtered and buried, my mother and father and I were not surprised: we knew now every particle of rain touches the face; everyone on earth is ours; anything on earth can happen.

Home, twenty-seven years and still so dangerous, but they come, refugees and recalcitrants, because they are less afraid of poisoned earth than poisoned cities, because they are safer in Belarus than they were in Tajikistan, Uzbekistan, Kyrgyzstan, the Caucasus.

Because strontium and cesium and plutonium
are invisible, and the guns of the soldiers

where we once lived, the spit and curse
of neighbors in Minsk and Kiev, the smoke
of fires and fumes of cars
in Moscow, the rocks of children—
these things we see. These things are real.

And look, there are houses here, collapsing,
yes, but we can fix them. The earth bestows.

Who can be afraid of roses
and raspberries?
Tell us, please: who can fear soil
and water, beets and squash—
apples, pears—
mushrooms, potatoes?

The cow looks thin, yes, but offers her body, shares
with us warm milk every morning.

Eat, here, please, sit with us
tonight, taste one sweet red tomato.

If our bodies feel strange, we call it joy. If our cells
feel full of light, we believe we are transfigured.

Let your dosimeters spin and beep.
What can numbers tell you? The eagle
eats the carp and flies so high above us.

Egret, owl, partridge, warbler—if falcons
don't fear voles, why should we refuse
the wheat, the cream, the glowing honey?

Yes, we know, the sarcophagus is cracking—yes,
we hear you: the hot heart of Chernobyl burns beneath it.

We know not how it hurts, but we can promise you this:
when the heart explodes again, we'll need no words:

the wind and the rain will tell us.

Listen: we promise: every body dies: blood and breath,
the same: and when we do, we die like animals.

23.

Twenty-seven years, and what surprises my mother and me
is the insistence of the garden: iris, lily: rain on the grass,
rain on the petals:

Tonight my father has disappeared in the rain, has gone out
in the rain looking for his brother, has seen Eamonn's face
behind rivulets of rain streaking the window, has heard his
brother's voice in wind through leaves—through rain on the
roof has heard Eamonn's hammer.

We can't call the police—the last time they came they
stunned him with tasers—afraid for themselves, they said—
he'd torn off his shirt and half-naked lurched toward them.

Eamonn, thirteen years gone, but alive tonight in the rain, in
my father.

My mother and I will drive these streets, search backyards
and alleys until we catch a thin, dangerous man shivering
in the rain, trembling in headlights—my father so cold and
confused he can't remember who we are or why he's out here.

> Another day sparks of perfect memory
> return: the smell of juniper, the taste
> of nasturtium, a girl shot in the throat—
> bloodroot, sweet pea, lilac, laurel—
> the cherry tree in bloom, the open mouth,
> the pink poppy—a man in a raccoon mask,
> radioactive rain, a cloud of birds,

fire, sarcophagus—his hands in his lap
too big for his body—everything here
and so clear, but he can't cling
to words, can't find the order.

The tattooed boy shows me doves fluttering across his back,
the body's grace where language fails.

24.

In a prison in California, a man who killed a woman a hundred times, who stabbed face and throat, heart and belly, who soaked himself in blood and rendered the body beneath his own unrecognizable, now washes another man in the shower, shaves his face, changes his diapers, protects and serves a murderer like himself, riddled by dementia—*blood everywhere, her eyes in my hands, she called me sweetheart*—knows repentance not as the hour of remorse, but as patience, surrender, a lifetime's work, the choice, the freedom, *now*, turning toward love every moment.

Brother, no one on this earth is unworthy of forgiveness
(killed her a hundred times)

no matter what you've done, there is a path, love
(rendered the body)

a way to become, to return to the self
(eyes, hands, heart) to be human.

I dream you in a place like this, alive all these years, given back this choice, this freedom, offered the gift, the blessing of purpose—I see you bathing a man old as our father, standing with him beneath a sharp spray of water, thanking him, washing his withered flesh, safe and saved, thanking the water, each of you unafraid, each in his own way healed—the beatitudes inscribed—not as words, but as actions.

Every body dies, yes, and when we do, we die like animals.

25.

Brother, tonight I lie awake in the rain and feel your breath, the rain, your heart inside me. Tonight while we lie dying in the rain, time spins backward, and the girl is rising up, unwounded, so graceful we can't believe, a puppet with limp legs pulled by strings, strong but too fine to see, utterly transparent.

If she's scared of you, a jittery, jumpy boy in a raccoon mask and hooded sweatshirt—if she's nervous, if she smells adrenaline pumping off your body, if she's disgusted by your filth, she will not show it.

The homeless men drift in and out of the store every day, every hour, and she looks away while they fill their pockets with Mallomars and bags of peanuts. She says, I'm about to dump the coffee, make a new pot—take what's there if you want it—and they do—five creams, six sugars—and she loves them for their hunger—Emily Ryan, this girl who sings so beautifully in choir, whose clear soprano voice could surge and soar, but she holds the voice back, lets it rise and fall, lets it be with the others—baritone, tenor—not one alone, but one of many—lets the voices of all move through blood and bone, pelvis, sacrum—this girl who believes sound more than sense, the trembling body—who loves her body when she sings, this holy place, this vessel where the voices of men and the voices of women and through them the voice of God enter, where her voice is one and all and God is inside and everywhere around her, infinite God overfilling her body, and nothing is not God, not sound, not whole, not part of her.

Sometimes, when she sees the men, their raw skin, their sharp bones, she wants them to sing with her, to know love as sound, their own perfection.

The women scare her more, jittery reflections of herself, unnamed possibilities, Aunt Avila locked in the house by Uncle Jude, a bolt too high for her to reach—because she goes, because she wanders—because he finds her leaning to the water—but the girl wonders which comes first: the locked door, or a woman's madness.

Brother, the video stops and starts and spins, and now it is the night before, and the girl lies on her bed, on the flowered quilt as old as she is, blue and green, rose and violet, each silk square stuffed and stitched (with all my love) *by Aunt Avila.*

Above her, a mobile strung with ninety-nine paper cranes swirls, faded birds folded by her mother, one a day for ninety-nine days (waiting for you to come into the world). *Inside each bird, a single word, a prayer, moonlight and rain, written by her father.*

Brother, what we hear now is the absence of human voices. Pine, wind, wolf, lily. We are unfolding the birds in the rain, letting the rain be the rain, letting the rain tear them, letting the rain wash the words:

----

we are making poems of the words

----

we will need no more words

ever

acknowledgments

I am grateful to the Lannan Foundation for providing sanctuary and support in Marfa, Texas.

I am also grateful to the National Endowment for the Arts; Corby Skinner and the Writer's Voice Project in Billings, Montana; the Utah Arts Council; Bob Goldberg and the Tanner Humanities Center; and the University of Utah. The faith of these individuals and the support of these institutions have made my work possible. Thank you.

I thank my family for their unwavering belief, their extraordinary contributions to research, their joyful reading and patient listening. Dear Gary, Glenna, Laurie, Wendy, Tom, Melinda, Kelsey, Chris, Mike, Sami, Brad, Hayley—Dear Mom, dear Father even now and always—Dear Cleora, Randy, Alicia, Valerie, Kimmer, Kristi—Dear Jan and John: without your love, there are no stories. Thank you.

To my students who teach and transform me, thank you.

The blessing of my agent Irene Skolnick's friendship and devotion has upheld me for twenty-eight years. Thank you.

To the editors of the journals where fictions, lyric essays, and poems from this project first appeared—*Five Points, Agni, Ocean State Review, Pleiades, Gulf Coast, Puerto del Sol, Shadowbox, SmokeLong Quarterly, Rock & Sling, The Elixir, Image: A Journal of the Arts and Religion, Orion, American Short Fiction*, and *Lumina*—thank you.

I am grateful to the board members, interns, and staff of FC2, Daniel Waterman, Vanessa Rusch, JD Wilson, Courtney Blanchard, Kristi Henson, Claire Lewis Evans, and the staff at University of Alabama Press. Thank you.

Special thanks to Steve Halle and the Publications Unit at Illinois State University for their elegant work and exquisite attention to detail.

For the faith and companionship, insight and inspiration of my early readers—Lance and Andi Olsen, Kate Coles, Mary Pinard, Betsy Burton, Paisley Rekdal, and Michael Mejia—I am endlessly grateful.

Dear Wendy, I must thank you again for sharing every part of this adventure, listening to every line, and for being so beautifully present that day when we discovered the evidence and understood at last how time moves at different speeds in both directions.